CRIME OF CONVEYANCE
HELEN GRAY
Ozark Hills Homicide, Book 2

ISBN: 978-1-0882-5216-1

Ginger Brewer pulled into the sparsely occupied lot of one of Springfield, Missouri's large medical buildings that housed a variety of physician's offices. She parked her blue mini-van and exited it into the March air that had a nip to it. The wind whipped her hair around her face.

Misgivings hummed through her as she entered the eerily quiet building and approached the pharmacy located at the right side of the lobby. It was the end of the business day, and the three people she had seen in the parking lot must have been the last stragglers to exit the building.

The pharmacist, Martha Peterson, had requested that Ginger meet her at the end of her shift, conveying the impression that she wanted privacy to discuss whatever was on her mind. She had sounded troubled.

As the director of Ozarkian Home Health Care, Ginger worked closely with a number of pharmacists in the area and kept in close communication with them. Her thoughts chased along different lines as she approached the partially open window in front of the druggist's counter and didn't see Martha in the portion of the room that was visible.

Irritation rubbed slightly at Ginger as she tapped on the Plexiglas shield across the front of the area while waiting for

Martha to respond. After all, she was the one who had called this meeting. But as moments passed, impatience turned to concern. Martha had sounded upset. Had she been called away suddenly? Was there an emergency? Was she in trouble?

Ginger leaned over and did a visual inspection of the room. When she still didn't see or hear anything or anyone, she pulled her phone from her purse and dialed Martha's cell phone. She had the number because she and Martha had gotten well acquainted during the time Martha's mother had spent in home health care and hospice before her death.

As the phone went unanswered, Ginger realized the ring was echoing from somewhere beyond the window. Holding the phone to her ear, she walked to the door at the left of the counter and turned the knob. To her surprise, it swung open.

Cautiously, not knowing what to expect, she stepped inside the pharmacy, glancing over her shoulder in one direction and then the other to see if anyone had entered the lobby from down the hallway or from the front parking lot. The lobby remained empty.

Her heart beginning to thump, Ginger edged forward, toward where the ring seemed to be originating. She rounded the end of the counter—and gasped at the sight of Martha lying crumpled on the floor, blood pooled around her head.

Ginger dropped to her knees next to the woman, let the phone fall beside her, and reached beneath Martha's heavy fall of long hair to probe her neck for a pulse. There was none. Rocking back on her heels, Ginger snatched the phone back up off the floor and dialed 911.

Tears leaked from her eyes and trailed down her cheeks as she sat waiting the few minutes before sirens could be heard arriving at the building. She couldn't comprehend how anyone could do something like this to another human being. Martha was a conscientious and dependable worker, friendly and always willing to go out of her way to assist clients or offer help to friends in need. It made no sense.

Yes, it did.

Martha worked with drugs. Thieves went to great lengths—even murder—to steal drugs. A shudder wracked Ginger as images of what Martha must have endured flashed through her mind.

Her thoughts were interrupted by the arrival of a pair of EMTs, followed closely by two police officers, and a man in a business suit not far behind. Tall and dark haired, with an air of authority, the man strode around the counter to where Ginger had stepped away from Martha to allow them access. His intense gaze focused on her.

"I'm Detective Jonathan Zalinski," he introduced himself. "You made the call?"

She nodded. "I'm Ginger Brewer."

He crouched next to Martha's body, pulled out a digital camera, and began taking pictures. Then he and the two uniformed policemen began a quiet conversation as the EMTs informed them that the woman was dead and stood aside to await the coroner's arrival.

Ginger stood in silence, feeling helpless and useless. For some reason, she couldn't tear her gaze away from the detective.

"The victim hasn't been here long," he said, turning from his picture taking to address Ginger. "How did you happen to find her?"

"She had called and asked me to meet her here as soon as she closed for the day. She sounded troubled," Ginger added, wanting to clarify the situation. "I was right on time, but she wasn't here—or didn't seem to be. I tried to call her and got no answer. But then I heard a phone ringing back here and came inside. I tracked the sound and found her. She's still warm, and this place would have been busy right up until closing time. She couldn't have been …killed more than a few minutes before I arrived."

"That's what the EMTs said. Who is she?"

"She's Martha Peterson, the pharmacist."

He glanced around the room. "Do you have any idea what happened here, who might have done this?"

Ginger shook her head. "Martha isn't …wasn't the kind of person who made enemies. The only thing I can think of is that someone forced their way in here to steal drugs."

His expression became grim. "There are too many addicts around to ignore that possibility."

~

Jon eyed the rack of shelving that had been knocked over. Bags of prescriptions that had been prepared for pickup by patients lay strewn across that section of the room, definite signs of a struggle. But the bags of drugs hadn't been taken. Maybe a robbery had been interrupted by the arrival of the health center director, a scary thought.

Ginger Brewer looked too professional—and attractive—to be caught up in something like this. She was short, maybe five foot if she stood on her tiptoes, with red hair that reflected blond highlights, and she wore neat gray slacks and a loose white top. But her husky voice didn't match her delicate appearance. And, before he'd put a few steps of distance between them, he'd gotten a whiff of summer flowers that had made his heart jump.

It bothered him. He had no interest in forming a relationship with any woman. He was happy as a bachelor, free to devote his full attention and time to his job. He was fortunate that Kelly had rejected him a couple of years ago for a more nine-to-five kind of guy. It had been a mistake for him to even consider marriage, an institution in which he held little confidence in light of his parents' tragic history.

"Do you know who will have to inventory this mess and determine if anything is missing?" he asked, forcing his mind back onto the business at hand.

The redhead's face crumpled, but she quickly regained her composure. "Martha would have done that. She maintained a meticulous inventory and kept track of details."

"What kind of people did she deal with regularly in her

job?"

"She worked closely with dispensers and sales associates. And there are others, like me, who pick up prescriptions for their clients."

"What kind of clients?"

"I'm the director at Ozarkian Home Health Care."

He nodded. "I get the picture." He also knew the strip mall location of that facility.

The victim had severe head trauma. He needed an opinion from the coroner as to what kind of weapon had caused it. He also needed to find her family and notify them of her death. "Do you know this woman's address?"

"Not offhand. I know the street where she lives, but I don't remember the number. I can call someone who'll know."

He was sure she understood, but he said it anyhow. "Don't say why you want it. I need to process the crime scene and notify her family before any information is released."

~

Ginger called her best friend Erin Stuart, asked for the address, and was given the information without being questioned. Erin was also a professional who dealt with patient confidentiality. Ginger disconnected and gave the detective the street number. Then she stood motionless, still trying to absorb what had happened, and watched them secure the scene and proceed with the processing and documentation that included the lobby as well as the entire pharmacy. If it hadn't been for the tragic circumstances, she would have enjoyed seeing them measure distances, angles and trajectories and search for trace evidence.

"You're free to leave," the detective said, approaching her during a pause. "I'll take care of business and stop by your office in the morning to take a more formal statement. You will be there, won't you?"

She nodded. "What time should I expect you?"

"What time do you get there?"

"Eight."

"Then I'll be there at eight."

Once at home in her apartment, Ginger took a leisurely bath, dressed for bed, and turned on the television. The detective must have already notified Martha's family, because the story was just breaking on the local news.

When the newscast ended, she turned off the set and sat staring at the blank screen. This afternoon she had spoken to Martha, a hard working single parent who was now a murder statistic. It was almost as shocking as Aaron's death. A car accident had claimed his life just as suddenly, only two weeks before they were to have been married. That had been six years ago, but it seemed a lifetime.

She went to bed and was just about to fall asleep when the land line next to the bed rang. She reached over, fumbled for it, and murmured a groggy, "Hello."

"Sorry I caught you sleeping," Erin said. "I'll call back …"

"No, I wasn't sleeping …yet," she amended, cutting off her friend's apology. "I assume you called about that news report."

"Well, you did ask for the woman's address."

Ginger rolled over onto her back, the phone to her ear, and explained her role in the episode. After covering that subject, she asked, "Are you about ready for your wedding?"

An optometrist, Erin had been caught up in a crime situation this past summer and fallen in love with the agent handling the case. They planned to marry in June.

"The plans are set," her friend assured Ginger. "But I have another project. Would you be interested in attending some auctions with me to look for items for the Christian theater? My folks have been big supporters of it for years, and they need to replace some furniture and smaller items they use for sets."

Ginger smiled. Erin's parents were now retired, but her

dad had spent most of his life as a pastor. They still participated actively in church, but the Christian theater here in Springfield had become their community involvement. "It sounds like fun."

"Good. I've heard people talk about treasures they've found at storage unit auctions. There's one Saturday that I think I'd like to attend. Miles says I can drive his truck, but he'll come help us load it if we buy anything we can't handle. I'll pick you up about seven-thirty Saturday morning." That would be day after tomorrow.

After their chat, Ginger was calmer and finally able to fall asleep.

The next morning, Detective Zalinski arrived promptly at eight and was shown to her office by Lillian, the receptionist. He took a seat near Ginger's desk and pulled a pen and notepad from his pocket. His cool dark gaze sent her heart into a tiny flip and made her pulse jump. It should be a crime for any man to look that good.

She placed her hands on the desk before her. "I've already told you everything I know."

"I understand that. But we're looking for details you might have missed when you were under stress. You were the only person on the premises when you found the body. Is that right?"

She nodded, replaying the scene in her mind. "There were only three or four people getting into their cars in the parking lot before I went inside. The lobby was empty. And no one was visible in the pharmacy when I walked up to the window."

He jotted notes as she spoke. "That was in spite of the fact that you had an appointment with the victim?"

"Yes. It irritated me a bit," she admitted, regretting that flash of emotion. "When Martha didn't appear after I tapped on the window, I called her cell phone. It took a couple of rings for me to realize that I was hearing more than just the sound from inside my phone. It was coming from the back part of the room."

"So what did you do next?"

She took a deep breath and repeated the sequence of how she had found the door unlocked, entered, and located Martha.

When she finished, the detective looked up from note writing, his gaze penetrating. "I understand you knew the victim personally. Do you know if she had any enemies?"

Ginger's head rotated back and forth. "I don't know of any, and I can't imagine that she did. She was a peaceful sort of person."

"What about romantic relationships?"

Ginger went silent, thinking. Then she shook her head. "I don't recall hearing Martha mention anyone, and there was never anyone with her when she spent time with her mother during the months she was a home health client with us before commencing hospice care."

When he sat studying her for long, intense moments, Ginger became uneasy. "I hope you don't think I would have done anything to Martha."

He shook his head. "I did a background check on you, and there's nothing that makes me believe you're anything other than what you say. That's correct, isn't it?"

The twitch at the corners of his mouth helped her relax. "What you see is what you get," she said with a shrug.

He tucked his notepad back in his pocket. Then he extracted a card from his wallet and handed it to her. "Here's my number, in case you think of anything you feel might be relevant." Then, instead of leaving, he leaned forward, a somber expression coming over his face. "I'd like to know more about home health and hospice care."

Ginger stared at him, unable to correlate the relevance. "Are you concerned that there was something questionable about the care Martha's mother received?"

"Oh, no, this is personal," he said, a raspy quality entering his voice. "I'd like to know more about such services, how they're arranged and managed."

He was asking about care for the terminally ill. "Does someone need such care?"

He nodded. "I do."

Chapter 2

"I mean my grandmother does, or will soon," Jon added as soon as he realized from her startled expression what he had made her think.

Seeming to relax a bit, Ginger picked up a pen. "Our agency only does home health, but we work closely with some hospice services."

"Can you set me up with both you and one of them?"

She nodded. "If you'll give me your grandmother's doctor's name, I'll pass it along so they can consult with him or her regarding your grandmother's needs."

"She uses Doctor Herbert Winkler. Thank you for doing this."

After jotting the name on her notepad, she leaned forward on the desk. "The hospice team will be on call twenty-four-seven, but our home health workers will provide the day-to-day care that includes such services as running errands, preparing meals, light housework, and assisting with hygiene. How soon do you want these services to start?"

"Immediately."

He forced himself to stop wondering how the lovely director, who he estimated to be near his thirty years of age, could still be single, having noted her bare ring finger. He listened as she outlined the nursing, resources, and emotional support their RN case manager and hospice aides provided.

"I'll get right on it then and call you as soon as we both have our paperwork ready. Respite relief care for caregiver exhaustion is also available," she added.

"That would be me," he said, feeling a measure of relief. "I moved back in with Gram and Gramps a couple of years ago. He lost his battle with cancer six months later, and since then Gram has suffered a massive stroke and been dependent on me. I have a widow lady from the church that stays with her some, but she's elderly and limited in how much she can handle Gram. I'm at the point where I can't give her the time she needs and keep working. Gram doesn't want to go into a nursing home, and I can't afford to give up my job. I spend as much time at home with her as I can, but additional health issues are making it clear that the …well, the end is near," he finished lamely, unable to verbalize the word death.

His grandparents were all he had ever had. Losing Gramps had been a really rough time for them. The thought of losing Gram as well tore him apart. They had raised him after the tragedy that ended the lives of both his parents. He owed them so much.

Jon read compassion in the director's eyes—and reached a decision. "I've spoken to another person or two, but tonight I'm going to tell Gram that I've signed her up with you and the hospice people. Thank you for your time. I'll be in touch about this—and the case."

He went to his vehicle, carrying the director's image with him. He shouldn't be noticing the blond tint to her red hair or the specks of gold in her blue eyes that made his heart beat a little faster. He had to stay focused on the case. Being a cop was tough on families, and he had made the choice of his work over marriage and a family.

He had to catch a killer. Even if he wanted it, he didn't have time for a love life.

As soon as he arrived at the station, Jon began reading

back over the research he had done on the victim, hoping to get an idea who would have had reason to harm her. The two things in Mrs. Peterson's personal life that stood out to him were a teenage son who had been in some trouble and the fact that she had an ex-husband somewhere. Could the son have been trying to steal drugs from his mother's pharmacy?

By the end of the day, he had established that the ex-husband was a truck driver and had been on a long haul, with his verified whereabouts in Kansas making it impossible for him to have killed Martha.

The son had been in school all day, and his fourteen-year-old sister said he had driven her home from school and been there with her, waiting for their mother to get in from work when the police arrived with news of her death. The seventeen-year-old boy had spent the past two days of school in ISS for food fighting in the cafeteria, but was allowed to drive to school today, and grounded after arriving home.

~

After the detective left, Ginger spent the day going about her daily routine, but the past eighteen hours hovered in the back of her mind, replaying over and over—when it wasn't veering back to Detective Jonathan Zalinski.

Late in the afternoon, one of their in-home workers entered the office, her face flushed and her long dark hair disheveled. "I'm running late," Katie said breathlessly. "I have paperwork to finish here, but I'm due at Mrs. Haskell's house at four, and I need her prescriptions from the pharmacy." Katie was new, but learning fast and doing a good job.

Ginger reached for her purse. "I'll run get the medicines while you do your paperwork."

Ironically, the prescriptions were at the same pharmacy where Martha had worked. Ginger fought a case of the shudders as she drove there and parked in the lot facing the building. Then she pulled herself together and went inside. Not sure what to expect, she was pleasantly surprised to find the pharmacy open. The woman in the middle of the room looked up as Ginger approached the counter. It was Lucy Thomas, Martha's assistant.

Lucy placed the item she was examining onto a shelf and approached Ginger. "Whose meds do you need?"

"Bonnie Haskell. How are things going?"

Lucy winced. "Okay, I guess. The police finally finished in here late last night. I spent the morning cleaning and putting things back in order—after the police had me search through Martha's records for them."

"Were drugs missing?"

Lucy shook her head. "If they are, it's only particular ones, or some I don't know about for some reason. I can't understand why Martha was …" A hand went over her mouth as tears glistened in her eyes. She was near Ginger's age, but dwarfed Ginger's four-foot-eleven height by six inches. Her hair was a light shade of brunette.

"I can't understand it either," Ginger agreed.

Lucy went to a shelf, plucked a paper bag off it, and brought it to the counter. "This is Mrs. Haskell's."

Ginger signed for it and left the building. When she slid behind the wheel of her minivan, she placed the bag and her purse on the passenger seat. Then she paused, picked up the bag, and opened it. Inside were two bottles, one of liquid laxative, the other of pills. Impulsively, she took out the pill bottle, thinking about the kind of drugs an addict would want to steal.

This particular prescription was for gabapentin, a drug not commonly thought of as one of abuse and not on the list of controlled substances. Its properties, however, were similar to many commonly abused intoxicants and were known to produce withdrawal symptoms and psychoactive effects.

As Ginger considered the low probability of addicts targeting it, she shook the bottle—and was surprised at the light weight and sound of it. She couldn't open it, but wondered if it possibly held the hundred pills indicated on the label. Were orders being shorted? Could that be what Martha had wanted to talk to her about?

While she mulled the long shot odds, Ginger's attention was drawn back to the present by the sight of a delivery van pulling up beside her. The driver emerged and loaded her arms with a stack of packages and well-sealed boxes from the back of the van. As she did, a box slid off the top of the stack and landed at her feet.

Ginger dropped the gabapentin back in the bag and exited her vehicle. "I'll get that for you."

The familiar driver smiled. "Thanks. This is quite a load. But it's no more than usual. I guess I'm just clumsy today."

Ginger returned the smile. "Everything is ordered online and delivered by mail or a service like yours these days. The volume of business has to be daunting."

"It sure is." The woman headed to the entrance of the building, her 'daunting' load balanced beneath her chin.

Ginger climbed back into her car, but paused before turning the key in the ignition. She pulled her phone and the card the detective had given her from her purse and dialed the number.

~

When Jon's phone rang, he noted the caller and answered quickly, a tad alarmed at hearing from Miss Brewer so soon. "Zalinski. What can I do for you?"

"I just picked up a prescription, and I don't think it feels right."

"Where are you?"

"On the parking lot of the pharmacy."

"You mean the one where the pharmacist was murdered?"

"Yes."

"Sit tight. I'll be there in five minutes."

When he pulled up beside Ginger's car in the parking

lot and beckoned for her to join him, she exited and slid into the passenger seat of his vehicle, a white paper bag clutched in her hand.

"Explain what you think you've found," he said as soon as she was settled, thinking what a nice profile she had. Smooth planes and angles. A firm jawline. Nicely shaped lips. None of which he should be noticing, he reminded himself, as the scent of her shampoo teased his senses.

She turned her head toward him, and for a moment her deep blue eyes gleamed captivatingly at him. Then she blinked and faced forward, making him wonder if she could possibly be feeling the same tug of attraction he was.

She withdrew a prescription bottle from the bag and handed it to him. "Feel the weight of that," she said, sounding as if she was struggling to keep her tone light.

He shook it, but didn't have an opinion. "How should it feel?"

"Like it has a hundred pills in it. I don't think it feels like it has that many, and I can't open a person's meds. Only the nurse or the patient can do that. It's an in-home patient," she explained. "I just picked up these prescriptions for the worker who's preparing to visit the woman's home to take care of her."

"Okay, call the nurse and have her meet us."

Her brow creased, but then she drew a long breath and called Elaine Knowles, the RN who worked for the hospice agency she had in mind for Jon. "She'll meet us at my office in twenty minutes," she said after disconnecting. Elaine was also a personal friend.

She returned to her car, and Jon followed her back to her office building in the strip mall that was populated by an assortment of boutiques and specialty stores. While she went inside, he scooted into her passenger seat and waited until she and the nurse exited. The nurse went to her own car, and Ginger placed a clipboard in the back seat before sliding behind the wheel.

"The Haskell home is only about a mile from here," she said. "We'll follow Elaine."

When they arrived at the house, they followed the nurse inside. Elaine opened the bottle in the presence of the elderly woman who sat in a wheelchair watching in puzzlement, and then she counted the pills and put them back inside the container.

Elaine frowned. "There are only half as many pills as there should be."

Ginger nodded. "I didn't think the bottle sounded or felt full enough and needed you to verify my suspicion."

The woman nodded. "I assume you'll talk to the pharmacist."

"Yes, I will," Ginger assured her. "Thanks for taking time to do this for me."

Once back in Ginger's minivan, Jon faced her. "Do you think this is connected to whatever got Mrs. Peterson killed?"

She started the motor, her expression pensive. "I don't know. I guess we need to know if it's an isolated instance, a simple error in packaging, or if orders are being routinely shorted. To be honest, I don't see how that could be."

"I assume the manufacturing process is streamlined and accurate, but even computers make mistakes occasionally." He gave her a wry look.

She nodded and steered into the street.

After reclaiming his police vehicle at the Ozarkian building, Jon returned to his own little office at the police department and called Miles Jarrett, a DEA agent who had worked a case in town weeks ago. Although Jon hadn't been the lead detective on that case, he had become acquainted with Miles during that time. After discussing the matter, Miles said he would do some checking and get back to him. Thirty minutes later he did.

"I talked to a manufacturer and then the head of a delivery service. In discussing their processes, each mentioned how well prescription drugs are monitored and packaged for delivery. They both think, since no other such abnormalities have been reported, that there has just been a computer glitch or some other unknown error that caused that particular prescription to be shorted. The patient will be issued an immediate shipment of the amount she was shorted. But it might be a good idea to have the home health and hospice care directors talk to their teams and establish a monitoring process."

After disconnecting, Jon called Ginger and relayed the information and suggestion.

~

"Are you awake yet?" Erin asked when she picked Ginger up Saturday morning. With her long honey-blond hair pulled back in a ponytail, her brown eyes were entirely too bright for such an early start to the day.

"I'm working on it," Ginger mumbled, raising her insulated coffee mug in a salute as she scooted into the passenger seat of the truck Erin was driving. They arrived at the row of self-storage units a few minutes before auction time and registered to bid. Then they viewed the contents, or what they could see of them, from the openings of the metal roll-up doors of the row of storage units. These were all either five by ten or ten by ten feet in size, with eight-foot ceilings. All the contents of the ones with SALE signs in front of them were to be auctioned. This was how owners recouped the loss of rental fees after a unit became delinquent.

Potential buyers could look inside the opened units, but they were not allowed to enter or touch anything. And payment was required immediately after any purchase.

The sounds of friendly chatter and occasional speculation on the value of certain items among bargain hunters were pleasant accompaniments to the day that promised to be warmer than the past few had been.

Ginger peered inside one of the bigger units and

pointed. "That looks like a nice sofa back there. And the clutter around it appears to be furniture that the theater could use."

The auctioneer began taking bids on the unit, and Ginger thought Erin was considering bidding when a scream erupted near the doorway. The crowd's attention was drawn to the scrawny looking woman who screamed again and pointed. "Rat! It's a rat!"

Erin faced Ginger, her expression matching the one Ginger was sure she also wore, wondering whether to laugh at the frantically gesturing woman or scream with her.

A man strode across the lot behind them. "What's going on here?" he demanded. He looked to be in his fifties, with a shock of salt and pepper hair and a muscular build. He wore tidy jeans, a blue polo shirt and a stern scowl. About medium height, he exuded an air of authority.

Ginger recognized Bob Caldwell, a well-known businessman who owned a string of storage units, apparently including these. He also served as a city councilman and tended to be quite vocal in his opinions on civic matters.

"Isn't he the owner?" Erin asked quietly while watching the man try to placate the woman, who continued to yell at him and fling accusations about the filthy condition of the place.

Ginger nodded.

"I think I've lost my urge for shopping," Erin said.

Ginger glanced around. "You're not the only one." People were beginning to drift away.

"I think estate sales would be better for what we want anyhow," Erin decided. "Let's go have brunch."

As unobtrusively as possible, they left and returned to Erin's vehicle. Minutes later they arrived at a restaurant whose specialty was a breakfast buffet.

Erin turned off the motor and faced Ginger. "I think we were just ratted out."

Ginger snorted. "I think you're right. But I'll bet you're

not too repulsed to eat."

"You think right."

They found a cozy booth in the restaurant and went to fill their plates.

"What do you think of the detective who's working Martha Peterson's murder case?" Erin asked after they were seated and had blessed their food.

Ginger thought about it before answering. There was something about him that drew her, but also something that warned her to keep her distance from him. He seemed dedicated to his job, but incredibly lonely, as if he distanced himself from others around him. "He seems focused and intelligent."

Erin's mouth twitched ever so slightly. "Miles says he's a good guy. They're friends. And the way Jon spoke of you in a discussion they had—something about the tone of his voice—made Miles think he's impressed with you."

Ginger studied her friend's face without comment.

"Miles says he's never known Jon to show interest in any woman. He has some hurts in his past and avoids women. He'd be a good match for you."

"He has some appeal," Ginger admitted, trying to sound nonchalant.

Erin grinned. "That's a start."

Ginger grinned back at her. "I think you're the rat."

Chapter 3

Ginger went to church Sunday, but only because her parents attended regularly and expected her to take them, as had become customary. And it was Mom's birthday. Ginger and her friend Erin had grown up in Ozark, a small town south of Springfield, and attended school and church together. They both lived in Springfield now, but still attended church with their parents.

Ginger had been a Christian since girlhood, but Aaron's death had erected a wall of anger between her and the Lord. She no longer prayed, having received no answer when she sat in Aaron's hospital room and begged God to keep him alive. She didn't understand why He had not protected Aaron from the drunk driver who had run through a red light and crashed into Aaron's truck, causing fatal injuries. Even worse, that drunk driver had walked away with only minor injuries.

Every time Ginger thought she had moved past the deep grief, something would happen that brought it back to the forefront of her emotions. The only thing she had found that blocked the pain from her mind was work, so she immersed herself in it. The one switch she had made was shifting from being an EMT to the home health care job. It was still a form of health care, but with better hours and less stress—most of the time.

After church, she and her parents went to Mom's favorite restaurant for lunch, and then back to their house for birthday cake that Ginger had baked and left in their kitchen when she picked them up that morning.

Monday morning, Ginger arrived at the office as the receptionist was unlocking the door. An older woman with grandchildren, Lillian was efficient, dependable, and related well with both workers and clients.

Together they entered the small reception area. A coffee table occupied the center of it, and four chairs were arranged about the room. Lillian's desk sat to the right of the entrance.

Ginger's office, located farther back and to the left, wasn't much bigger. It contained her desk, a couple of chairs, and three file cabinets. She stowed her purse in a lower drawer of her desk and began the workday by calling Lucy Thomas at the pharmacy.

"I'll call the drug company and see what I can find out," the pharmacist said as soon as Ginger finished explaining about the pill shortage. "But first I'll check the other containers from that order. I'll call you back when I know something," she promised. Concern was evident in her tense tone and clipped speech.

Ginger thanked her and disconnected. Then she composed a letter to the agency's employees outlining the need to monitor drugs for inconsistencies and describing precautions to take when picking up and delivering medications. When workers stopped by the office, they were given copies of the letter and cautioned to speak to no one but office personnel about the matter.

Ginger was sitting at her desk, pondering what to do next, when her phone rang. Absently, she reached for it. "Hello."

The sound of sobbing jerked her to attention. "Who is this?"

"Gi …Ginger," a woman stammered. "This is Ch …Ch

…Cheryl."

"Okay, pull yourself together," Ginger said gently, hoping to calm the upset in-home aide while glancing at the calendar on her computer screen to see Cheryl's schedule. A long-time employee, she had an excellent work record. "Are you at Mrs. Boswell's house?" she asked.

"No. I was," Cheryl added quickly, speaking a bit more coherently. She paused and drew an audible breath. "I did her grocery shopping, but when I got back and unlocked her apartment door to take them inside, a man ran up behind me and pushed me inside. Then he …" Sobs choked her for a few moments before she could continue. "He knocked me down. I hit my head on the door and blacked out for a minute or two. When I came to, I had trouble getting up, and I heard him beating Mrs. Boswell and yelling for her to tell him where she hid her money. He robbed her. And then he …he made me dr …drive him somewhere and get out of my car. Then he took my car and left me here."

"You're safe now. Can you tell me how to find you?"

Cheryl began to speak a little more calmly. "We left Springfield on the Kansas Expressway, but somewhere between there and Bolivar he made me turn onto a side road. Then we wound back into a remote spot, and he made me get out."

"Did you pass Willard?" The small town was about eight miles that direction.

"Yes."

"Do you remember any mile markers?"

"No. I was so scared I didn't notice." Her voice hitched.

"That's okay. Keep your phone in your hand. I'm going to disconnect and make a call. Then I'll head that way and call you right back."

"Thank you, Miss Brewer."

Ginger replaced the land line, grabbed her purse and windbreaker, and extracted her cell phone from the purse. "Cheryl needs help," she called to Lillian as she passed the reception desk, dialing Detective Zalinski while moving at a near run. "Get an ambulance over to Mrs. Boswell's house," she added, speaking over her shoulder as she rushed out the door.

As she reached her car, the phone rang in her ear. She yanked the driver's door open and tossed her purse inside.

"What's up?" Jon asked.

"I have a worker in trouble." She explained while holding the phone with one hand and pushing the other arm into the sleeve of her windbreaker. A strong gust of March wind whipped the rest of the garment behind her. She yanked the car door open and slid behind the wheel. Then she shrugged on into the windbreaker while explaining Cheryl's predicament. "Can you track her phone?"

"Yes," he replied briskly. "I'm only a mile or so from you. If you'll wait a minute, I'll swing by for you."

She quoted Cheryl's number quickly, closed the car door, and turned around. He had tracking ability. She didn't. "Okay. I'll be waiting at the entrance."

She disconnected and called Cheryl back while speed walking to the edge of the parking lot. "The detective and I are on our way to find you," she assured the employee. "I'll stay on the line with you."

Two minutes later, Jon's car pulled alongside her. "I've called in a report," he said as she vaulted into the passenger seat. "Backup is on alert if we need it."

It took a half hour for him to drive past Willard and find his way to Cheryl, while Ginger continued to talk to the woman and assure her they would find her.

When they turned onto a gravel road and followed it to a clearing where Cheryl stood, Ginger breathed a huge sigh of relief.

As soon as Jon stopped the car, she leaped out and hurried to her employee. The woman was clearly upset. She had a right to be. But, thankfully, the only injury she had was a large knot and bruise near the crown of her head from hitting the door when the thief struck her.

"Do you feel able to go to the police station with us?" Jon asked Cheryl. "I'd like to take your statement and have you see if you can identify the guy who did this."

"I'll do it whether I feel like it or not," Cheryl stated emphatically as he finished the question. "I want him caught." She faced Ginger. "Is Mrs. Boswell okay?"

"I told Lillian to send an ambulance to her house, but I haven't checked on her yet." She felt guilty that she hadn't already done that.

"She's in the hospital," Lillian said when Ginger asked about the woman. "I called her daughter, and she's with her. It sounds like she's going to be all right, but she has a lot of bruising and soreness."

Anger roiled inside Ginger that someone would abuse an elderly person that way. As she relayed Lillian's report, Cheryl's and Jon's expressions conveyed similar emotions.

Jon ushered Cheryl into the back seat of his police vehicle and drove directly to the police station. After Cheryl wrote out a formal statement, he placed an album of photographs before her. Then he and Ginger waited while the worker studied them.

Cheryl's face remained studious, but without recognition while she thumbed through several pages. But then she paused and leaned closer, peering intently at a particular photograph. Moments later she raised her head and pointed. "That's him."

Jon pulled the mug book across the table to him and turned it upright. "It's Jimmy Atkins. He's a known drug addict, so he was undoubtedly after drug money."

"Do you think he might have murdered Martha?" Ginger asked.

He heaved a long breath. "I don't know. But this certainly puts him on the suspect list."

~

Jon shuffled papers on his desk, looking for the note he

had made with Jimmy's last known address on it. He hadn't found the guy at home earlier, but he meant to go back to that run-down apartment building after the meeting he had returned to the department to attend. He would try to find the apartment manager, who had been invisible on that first visit.

He read over the reports on Jimmy, noting names of known cohorts. Then he shoved the papers back in the folder and went to his meeting.

The session lasted until five o'clock, but he wasn't going home. He called Gram's caretaker and was assured that his grandmother was okay. Then he drove back to Jimmy's apartment building. And got lucky. As he started to get out of his car, he spotted Jimmy ambling up the sidewalk. But instead of entering the store when he approached the main entrance, Jimmy paused and veered around the corner of the building.

Jon hopped out of his police vehicle and took off in pursuit. By the time he rounded the building, Jimmy had headed across the street. He didn't act as if he knew he was being followed, but he did quicken his pace and pull a phone from his pocket.

The thirtyish drug addict hoofed it up the street, putting his phone back in his pocket as Jon closed the space between them. At a discount store, he veered to the entrance. As he did, the door slid open automatically, and a man similar in age and stature exited. When they met, both guys came to abrupt halts. Then the guy who had just exited the store gave Jimmy a shove. And, of course, Jimmy shoved him back. An instant scuffle began.

"Hey!" Jon shouted, running to intervene.

The two men paused, shot him a glance, and then exchanged a look with one another. Then, in a sudden move, they both ran toward Jon. Almost simultaneously, one kicked at his left ankle, while the other landed a kick to his right knee, as if they had used the maneuver before.

Jon landed on his right hip on the sidewalk. By the time

he made it to his feet, gritting his teeth against the pain in his knee, the men had fled in opposite directions.

Frustrated, he limped back to his car and sat rubbing his knee until the pain subsided enough for him to drive. He glanced over at the Ozarkian Health Care Center as he rolled past it, tempted to pull in and talk to Ginger. But he didn't have a valid excuse to disrupt her routine, so he resisted the impulse and forced himself to focus on the investigating he needed to do.

He drove to the medical building where the pharmacist had been killed and began visiting other offices, hoping to learn which doctors had patients leaving from appointments at the time that would have had them passing through the lobby at the approximate time of the murder, with emphasis on those who had prescriptions to pick up at the pharmacy.

Hours later, each office had been visited and personnel interviewed. No one had seen or heard anything helpful, and no one had any idea who would have been in the lobby at that time. He did, however, have a couple of names of people who had been given prescriptions to be filled at that particular pharmacy.

~

Troubled and baffled, Ginger dealt with paperwork, handled phone calls, and searched client files for anything relating to pharmacy needs or records of other incidents resembling what had happened to Mrs. Haskell.

Late in the afternoon, she was weary, both physically and mentally. She shoved the papers to the edge of her desk and went to the little room where they had a small kitchenette for employee breaks. She took her personalized mug from the cup rack on the counter next to the coffee maker and poured it half full of the dark brew. Then she sank onto the love seat in the corner of the room and picked up the remote for the small TV that sat on the end of the counter. She pressed the On button, but muted it as Lillian entered the room, wiping at her eyes. The woman was impeccably dressed, as usual, in a blue skirt and white blouse. Her short, bob cut hair matched her brown eyes that were bleary with tears.

The receptionist halted. "Sorry to intrude. I didn't realize you were here," she said in a voice that vibrated with distress.

Ginger patted the cushion beside her. "I was too tired to accomplish much and decided to clear my head." She indicated the coffee mug.

Lillian nodded in understanding and sank down beside her. "My head hurts," she said softly. "Crying does that to me."

Ginger frowned, remembering. "You went to school with Martha Peterson, didn't you?"

Lillian nodded. "We were friends."

Ginger reached over, placed a hand over Lillian's, and squeezed it. "I'm so sorry. And angry," she added, being honest. "I want to see her killer caught. Do you have any idea what was going on in her life, personally or professionally, that could have led to such violence?"

Lillian shook her head, tears pooling in her eyes again. "I wish I did. It's so heartbreaking."

Ginger nodded. "I don't understand how God can allow such injustices." Instances like this always brought a renewal of grief and pain over Aaron's death.

Lillian drew a long, uneven breath. "We can't blame God."

"But He didn't protect Martha." *Or Aaron.* "Why?"

"I don't know." Lillian's expression held depths of sorrow. "But I know evil exists in this world. Can we pray together about it? That's what I came in here to do."

Ginger's mouth trembled. "I don't think I can. I've forgotten how."

"May I?"

She nodded, pain compressing her lungs to the point she would strangle if she tried to speak.

Lillian bowed her head. "Heavenly Father, please lead the police to the person who killed Martha. We place the matter in Your hands."

She gave Ginger's hand a final squeeze and stood. "I need to go on home and start supper for Fred. He's always starving when he gets home from work." She tried to speak lightly, but failed. "See you tomorrow."

When Lillian was gone, Ginger drained her mug, rinsed it, and put it back in place. Then she picked up the TV remote to turn off the set. But she paused as the news alert scrolling across the bottom of the screen caught her attention, something about a fatal accident.

As she tried to make sense of the message, having missed the beginning of it, an anchor of the local news station appeared on the screen, delivering a newly breaking story.

"Mrs. Williams fell from the balcony of her second-floor apartment and died from her injuries," the short-haired blond announced. "The incident happened shortly after lunch today. According to a family member, she often ate her lunch out on the balcony, and it is theorized that she dropped something while standing at the railing and fell over it while attempting to catch the item. A drink container was found on the sidewalk near her."

Ginger's heart ached for that poor woman's family. She started again to turn off the TV, but halted, her breath catching when a picture of the accident victim appeared on the screen. She stepped closer, studying the image to be certain. It was the woman who had made a scene at that storage auction.

When the picture disappeared, she completed the motion of silencing the TV. Then, her thoughts scattered, she returned to her desk, tidied it, and collected her purse to leave the office. As she locked the door, she tried to squash the feeling of unease that crept through her. Another murder may have just been committed in their city. Yes, that woman had been rude and obnoxious, but that didn't give anyone the right to kill her. If they had.

Preoccupied with questions, Ginger walked to her car, barely aware of her surroundings. As she approached the vehicle, she automatically pulled her keys from her purse and pressed the button to unlock the doors.

She gripped the door handle and pulled. As she did, she suddenly sensed a presence behind her. The next thing she knew, hands reached around her neck, clamped over her mouth, and caught her in a chokehold.

Chapter 4

Acting in sheer survival instinct, Ginger swung her right hand upward and stabbed at the hand below her chin. As the assailant grunted, she rammed her elbow backward into his ribs.

When the thug momentarily lost his balance, Ginger lunged sideways, terror squeezing the breath from her, and broke free. Not wasting a second, she burst into a run across the parking lot. Footsteps slapped on the paved surface behind her.

Help me, Lord. Please.

At that moment she heard a motor come to life farther up the lot. Then a car screeched away, while another car came rolling toward her.

"Are you all right?" an older gentleman asked as the driver's window of his vehicle lowered. "I was pulling into the other end of the lot and saw someone attack you."

Ginger ran a hand over her aching throat. "I'm okay," she rasped, feeling dizzy.

"I'll call the police," the Good Samaritan said.

She raised a hand. "I can do it. Will you stay here with me until I get help?"

The gentleman pushed his door open and grabbed her arm as she staggered. "You have to get off your feet."

Ginger let him guide her to a sitting position on the cold surface of the lot, shivering as a gust of wind swept through. She withdrew her phone from her purse that was miraculously still dangling from the strap over her left arm, and dialed Jon.

"I was attacked on our parking lot," she blurted as soon as he answered. "But I got away."

"Are you still there?"

"Yes."

"We'll be there in ten minutes."

She disconnected and looked up at her benefactor. "Thank you for coming to my aid. I think you just saved my life."

The man gave her a tight smile. "I'm glad God put me here at the right time. I came to pick up my granddaughter from her piano lesson." He nodded at the music store with a small studio in the back that was located a few doors down the strip mall. The lot had already emptied in most of the businesses. Ginger's office was at the lower end of the mall.

A police car, with lights flashing, roared up the highway and veered into the lot. A second cruiser followed right behind it. A grim faced Jon emerged from the first vehicle as soon as it jerked to a stop at the curb. A uniform clad officer emerged from the second car and joined him.

"Are you hurt?" Jon asked, dropping to a squat before her. His gaze raked over her in assessment, coming to rest on her throat.

Ginger shook her head. "I'm okay. This kind gentleman drove up, and the attacker fled."

Jon stood and gripped the older man's hand. "Thanks for stopping. Many would not have done so. Will you tell me your name and what you saw?" He pulled out a notepad and pen as he spoke.

The man nodded. "I'm Roger Hampton, pastor of East Side Community Church. I was coming to pick up my teenage granddaughter from her music lesson. A school friend brought her here after school, dropped her off, and went on home. Brianna's mother normally picks her up, but she had a doctor appointment this afternoon, and I said I'd come get her. When I turned into the parking lot entrance, I saw someone run up behind this lady and attack her. She jabbed him with something and rammed him with her elbow, throwing him off balance. As I drove down here, the jerk saw me and ran away."

Ginger raised her key in the air. "I stabbed him with this."

The slightest grin tugged at Jon's mouth, but only briefly. Then his attention returned to the gentleman. "Can you describe the attacker, or his getaway vehicle?"

The minister's face crinkled in concentration. "He wasn't a real big guy. He wore dark pants and a dark coat, with some kind of cap over his head. I only saw him from the back. The shoulders and hips were on the thin side. He was a few inches taller than the lady here."

"What about the vehicle?" John repeated when he paused.

The minister frowned. "I saw a white car pull out down there," he said, pointing toward the far corner of the lot, "but I was focused on the victim here. Sorry I can't tell you a make or model. I really need to go now. My granddaughter is waiting for me."

The other officer stepped nearer. "I'm Officer Delton Booker. Would it be okay if I follow you to pick up your granddaughter and take her home? Then we could go to the police station and take your formal statement. If that works for you," he added, addressing Jon.

Jon nodded. "Thanks, Del. And thank you, Pastor Hampton. I'll finish talking to Miss Brewer and see that she gets home safely."

As the pastor and officer left, Ginger couldn't help but wonder if God really had sent the pastor at the right moment. He thought so. Why would the God who had allowed Aaron to be killed and not answered her prayer for his survival spare her life?

Failing to understand, she looked upward. *If you did do that for me, thank you, Lord.*

"Why do you think this happened?"

Jon's question jerked her mind back to the present situation. She shook her head. "I have no idea."

"You found a dead body. Now you're attacked," he said, speaking in slow reflection. "I'm afraid whoever killed Mrs. Peterson thinks you saw or heard something that can identify him. If that's the case, you're in the crosshairs of a killer."

She licked her dry lips and started to stand. When she did, Jon gripped her forearm and assisted her upright. "Do you have some place you can go other than where you live?"

Unprepared for his touch, or the jolt of awareness that accompanied it, Ginger made a quick inhalation of breath, struggling to think. "My parents live south of here, between Springfield and Ozark, but I don't want to put them at risk."

"Do you have any other family in the area?"

"My younger brother's in the military and stationed overseas, and the older one lives in Iowa," she said, gathering her muddled thoughts. "But I have a close friend who would let me stay in her spare room."

"Call her. I'll follow you there to be sure you arrive safely."

"I need a few things, like clothes and toiletries. Could we go by my apartment so I can pack an overnight bag?"

He drew a deep breath. "Okay, but I'll be right behind you."

Ginger started toward her car, pulling out her phone. She dialed Erin Stuart. "I need a place to spend the night," she said when her friend answered. "I'll explain when I get there."

"Have you eaten?" Erin asked.

"No, but I'm not real hungry." To her embarrassment, her stomach growled, bringing a raised brow look to the detective's face.

"I have a pot of chili ready to eat, and there's over half a chocolate pie that I made last night. Are you sure you can't help me eat them?"

"I can." She glanced over at her escort. "By chance do you have enough for another person?"

"I do, but you better hurry. I'm hungry, and I want to hear what's happening with you."

"See you in a few minutes." Ginger disconnected and walked to her car. She opened the door and looked at the detective again. "Would you be interested in a bowl of chili and a piece of homemade chocolate pie?"

~

Jon was surprised at the invitation. "It sounds good," he admitted honestly. "I didn't get to have lunch."

"Then let's go."

As soon as she slid behind the wheel, he closed her door and hurried to his own vehicle. He followed Ginger to her apartment and waited on the sofa while she packed a bag. Then they drove to a house in another part of town. A woman he recognized as Erin Stuart opened the door as they approached the porch. She smiled.

Ginger and the woman embraced at the doorway, and then Ginger turned to him. "Jon, I think you may know my friend, Erin Stuart. Erin, meet Detective Jon Zalinski."

"I remember you," Jon said, reaching to shake her hand.

Erin's smile faded. "I also remember meeting you briefly when I was drawn into that drug case at the mall where I have my optometry practice."

He nodded. "I didn't deal with you personally, but I followed the case closely and was present on a couple of calls. So I feel like I know you."

Her smile returned. "Well, you can cross my doorsill now. Come on in and let me know how I can help Ginger. She helped me," she added, speaking over her shoulder as she headed across the room. "Ginger, leave your bag in here.

You can put it away after we eat."

Ginger edged over close to him. "Erin is engaged to the DEA agent who was working undercover as a security guard."

He nodded. "I remember hearing about that."

Everything was already on the table, including iced tea. After Erin said a brief blessing, she ladled chili into their bowls. She waited until dessert had been served to aim a direct look at Jon and then Ginger. "Okay, I'm ready to hear what's going on that has my friend scared out of her apartment."

Jon put his fork down. "She was attacked in the parking lot as she went to get in her car after work this afternoon."

Erin drew a swift breath, but otherwise remained calm. "Do you think it's related to her finding Martha's body?"

"I'm afraid so. The killer must think she saw or overheard something important enough to warrant silencing her." He hated the way his statement made Ginger's face go pale, but she needed to understand the severity of the situation.

"But I didn't," she protested, the quaver in her voice telling him that she was genuinely frightened.

Erin frowned, studying her. "I understand how you feel," she said in slow thought. "When I was in a similar situation, I eventually discovered details that had not been obvious before. When you're alone in a quiet place, you could recall something meaningful."

Ginger sat motionless, absorbing her friend's words. "I'll keep that in mind," she promised. "Right now all I can think about is what happened this evening."

Erin nodded, chewing and swallowing. "Had you just left the office when this happened?"

Ginger nodded. "Everyone was gone, even Lillian. She had been upset, and we talked in the break room before she left. Martha was a friend of hers."

Jon nodded in understanding. "So you talked, and then

both of you left?"

She began a nod, but stopped. "Well, Lillian left, and I started to turn off the television to follow her, but a breaking news story caught my attention. I watched it before leaving. It was about a woman falling off her balcony, and when they showed her picture, I recognized her."

"Do you mean the Williams woman?"

She nodded.

Surprise shot through him. "Delton and I were just leaving that scene when you called me. How do you know her?"

"I don't. Erin and I saw her at a storage shed auction."

Erin emitted a startled sound. "You mean the rat woman? She's dead?"

"Yes," Ginger said.

Jon looked at both of them. "Tell me why you remember her."

Now the two women exchanged glances. "She made a disturbance," Ginger said. "She started yelling and pointing and saying she saw a rat."

He squelched a snort.

"When the owner came and started talking to her, we left," Erin continued. "And it looked like a number of other people were doing the same thing."

"Was her death an accident?" Ginger asked.

"It looks that way."

Her gaze locked on his. "But you're not sure?"

He shrugged. "We're never sure about any case until we've examined it from every angle. Then, if we suspect anything in the way of foul play, we have to find proof. Now, let's get back to the attack on you. Does your agency have its own security camera, or do I need to contact mall headquarters about that?"

"The mall," she answered briefly.

~

Ginger didn't sleep well that night. Memories of being

attacked, the fear, kept replaying in her head. It was almost a relief when morning arrived so she could block the thoughts with physical activity. Erin already had omelets ready when she entered the kitchen.

"You don't look so good," her friend observed. "Couldn't sleep, huh?"

Ginger shook her head and dropped onto a chair at the table. They ate quickly and prepared to go their separate ways. When she heard a car pull into the drive, she peeked out the window and recognized the detective.

"You *will* be careful, won't you?" Erin urged as Ginger walked to the door, looping her purse strap over her shoulder. Genuine concern radiated from her. And if anyone understood, it was Erin, having experienced the trauma of being attacked.

"I will," Ginger promised, exiting the house. Having an escort to work beat being told she had to stay home. And, truth be told, she welcomed the measure of safety.

She scooted behind the wheel of her minivan and drove her normal route to work, with the detective's car close behind her. Only when she reached the office door of her agency and had it unlocked to enter did he wave and drive away.

Ginger had just settled at her desk when she heard Lillian enter. "I'll make coffee," the receptionist called from the front office.

Minutes later she entered Ginger's office, carrying two mugs with steam rising above them. She placed one on Ginger's desk and sat in a chair facing her, cradling her own mug in her hands. "How are you this morning?"

With reluctance Ginger told Lillian about the attack.

"Why would someone do that?" Indignation laced her question when Ginger finished.

"All I or the detective can figure is that Martha's killer thinks I can identify him. I spent the night with a friend. Jon followed me as I drove there, and then returned and escorted me here this morning."

The sound of her office phone ringing brought Lillian to her feet. As she scurried away, Ginger's cell phone dinged the arrival of a text. She pulled the phone from her purse. The message was from Jon.

Can you look at surveillance footage with me if I come get you in five minutes?

She texted back that she could and followed Lillian to the front. At the desk, she waited for the receptionist to get off the phone. "I'm going to look at surveillance film with the detective. I shouldn't be gone long."

Moments later Jon entered the room, nodded at Lillian, and escorted Ginger to his car. Within minutes they were seated in the mall's security office gazing at the footage.

Ginger held her breath when the attacker was shown darting up behind her and attempting to choke her.

"You made a good move with that key stabbing," Jon commented. "It shocked him and allowed you to get in that elbow jab. Is there anything familiar about the person?"

She peered at the image, studying it in detail. The guy's back was to the camera. He wore a dark coat and knit cap. Average height and muscular. Her head rotated back and forth. "There's nothing there that gives me a clue to who it could be."

"Okay, I'll take you back to your office."

As he finished speaking, his cell phone rang. "Zalinski," he answered.

Ginger couldn't hear the other side of the conversation, and Jon's comments were mostly brief yeses or noes, followed by a thank you for calling. When he disconnected, he faced her.

"That was Lucy, the murder victim's assistant who is now in charge of that pharmacy. I asked her to check on that bottle of pills you said contained only half what it should have held. She checked and found that all the bottles in the package that bottle was part of were only half full. Then she checked with the drug company and was told that there apparently was some kind of glitch in their system. They're taking full responsibility and sending replacements of the entire order."

Jon moved as if to stand, but then settled back in the chair. "How did you end up in the work you do?"

The personal nature of the question took her by surprise. "It was a career switch. I was an EMT working crazy hours. The night shifts were rough, mostly because I couldn't sleep during the daytime. I found a job that's still health care, but with daytime working hours and less stress. Until now."

"That makes sense," he said quietly. His voice held an odd quality that made her heart beat a little faster.

When he stood and held out a hand, she placed hers in it and let him tug her to her feet.

He glanced from her hand to her face. And his pupils dilated as their gazes met. When his eyes traveled over her features and came to rest on her mouth, the scrutiny made her lips tingle.

Her heart thudded in her chest, while disjointed thoughts whirled through her mind. They had only met days ago. It was crazy to be thinking about kissing him. But when he traced his fingertips along the line of her jaw and tucked a stray strand of hair behind her ear, she stepped nearer.

As his head began to lower toward hers, footsteps sounded at the doorway. He stepped back, the tenuous thread between them broken.

Chapter 5

"This is Mike Edwards, the security guard," Jon said as the uniformed guy entered the room, mentally kicking himself for his lapse in focusing on the job.

The guard extended a handshake to Ginger. "I've seen you around, but we haven't spoken. Sorry about what happened to you."

She nodded. "Glad to meet you. Thanks for this." She indicated the computer screen with a head motion.

"I'll take you back to your office now," Jon said as the guard claimed the seat at the computer that had just been vacated.

After dropping Ginger at her office, he drove back to his own department. At his desk, he called home. "How's Gram?" he asked when Mrs. Hamlin answered, worry eating at him. When he got up that morning and checked on his grandma, she had seemed confused and feverish. Mrs. Hamlin had promised to call her doctor, and Gram had been alert enough to order Jon to go on to work. He had left, but would return home if necessary.

"I sponged her like the doctor told me and gave her the medicines he said to give her. She's resting now."

Relief flooded him. "Thank you, Olive. I don't know

what I'd do without you."

"I'll call you if she seems worse again," she promised.

Jon thanked her again, disconnected, and bowed his head. *Help me, Lord. I don't want to lose her, but I can't bear to see her suffering.* The only peace he had was the knowledge that she looked forward to joining Gramps in heaven.

He swallowed his grief and stared at the stack of reports on his desk, debating what to tackle first. When his phone rang, he answered absently. "Zalinski."

"I got a tip where Jimmy Atkins has been seen," Delton said briskly.

"Where are you?" Jon left his chair as he spoke.

An hour later, they arrested the strung out Jimmy at a bar where he had caused a ruckus when the bartender refused to serve him. An informer of Delton's had happened to be present and texted him.

Once Jimmy was behind bars for robbing and attacking the elderly woman, Jon decided to check on the two people whose names he had obtained from personnel in doctor offices as persons who had been given prescriptions to pick up near the time of Martha's death. Neither of them, a young mother with a toddler, and an elderly gentleman, seemed likely suspects.

Back at his desk later, Jon sat thinking back over recent happenings and conversations. He somehow found his mind bouncing back to Mrs. Tanya Williams and wanting to know more about her. He did some research and was pondering what to do next when the coroner called. "Mrs. Peterson had a large contusion and bruising near the crown of her head, and she was stabbed in the chest with what I'd guess to be a knife, but not a very sharp one," the physician reported.

When the call ended, Jon went to the chief's office and leaned inside the doorway. "I'm going to go talk to that pharmacist again, the assistant who took the murdered woman's place. Hopefully she can help me figure out what kind of weapon caused Mrs. Peterson's wounds. When I'm done, I need to check on Miss Brewer and then go home."

"How's your grandma?" the chief, who was in his sixties and nearing retirement, asked.

"Not good." Emotion clogged his throat.

"If you need to be with her, do it. Just give me a call if you need anything. Okay?"

Jon gave him a brief nod and left. The chief knew his circumstances and that the time Gram had left on earth was growing short. The home health worker was to begin visiting today, but she would be more help to Mrs. Hamlin than Gram.

When Jon approached the pharmacy window, he spotted Lucy at one side of the room. When she looked over and recognized him, she immediately put down the prescription bottle she was labeling and walked toward the door. Moments later, the lock clicked, and the door opened. "Come in, Detective," she invited, widening the opening.

"Is something wrong," she asked when he was inside, the door relocked. She didn't appear or sound overly worried, yet there was a degree of tension in her body language and tone.

He scanned the room, looking for possible weapons of opportunity. "The coroner says Martha has a large contusion on her head and a stab wound in her chest that looks like it was caused by something not very sharp. Do you have any idea what could have caused them?"

The woman frowned, her head beginning to rotate in a visual inspection of the room. Then she began to walk slowly along the back of the counter. When she reached the far end, she paused, obviously deep in thought.

Jon kept silent, not wanting to break into whatever mental connection she might be making.

Continuing to scan the room, Lucy walked to the back section, scanning it in detail. Shaking her head, she returned to the front and paused at the counter. Then she opened a drawer beneath the center of the counter and studied the contents. At first, she seemed blank, but then she began to rake her hand around inside it, reaching back into the rear. She rechecked the entire drawer.

When she looked up, her expression radiated uncertainty. "I think there should be another knife in here," she said slowly. She stepped over to where she had been working when he arrived, picked up a tool and held it up for his inspection.

"It's a stainless-steel knife spatula," she explained. "We ordinarily have two of them, in case Martha and I, or anyone else, needs to count pills at the same time. But this is the only one I see here now. I haven't been too observant lately," she apologized.

"I understand," he said gently. And he did. The violent death of the woman who had most likely been her mentor had shaken her. He pulled out his phone. "May I take a picture of that?"

"Of course." She held the tool suspended between two fingers.

Jon snapped a picture. "Thanks. You've been a big help."

When he returned to his SUV, he sat motionless behind the wheel, debating for a few moments. He hadn't taken time for lunch. It was getting late in the day, but not late enough for the home health office to close. He didn't want to go back to headquarters, and he wasn't about to go home without knowing that Ginger had made it safely to her friend's house. He decided to visit her and give an update on Gram. He started the motor.

~

Ginger looked up when Jon entered her office.

"Your receptionist told me to come on in," he said, walking over and dropping onto the chair facing her desk. "Do you have time to chat with me?"

She tucked the work applications she had been

reviewing back into a folder and shoved it aside. "It's actually a good time. What's on your mind?"

He ran a hand over his chin. "How is your worker who was abducted after her client was robbed? And how is the elderly client recovering from her beating?"

"Cheryl is back at work, and the client is improving from the beating. But they both want to see the perpetrator caught."

"He was arrested this morning."

"So he's in jail?"

Jon nodded. "But he demanded a lawyer and refused to say anything. So we're stalled on that case. I've made a wee bit of progress on the murder case, though."

Ginger listened as he told her about the coroner's report, talking to Lucy at the pharmacy, and learning that she thought a spatula was missing.

"The killer hit her in the head with a weapon he had with him," she theorized, "but maybe he dropped it, and then grabbed the spatula and stabbed her. Afterward, realizing it would be evidence, he took it with him."

"The stabbing might have happened first, and then she was finished off with the head bashing," Jon offered, agreeing with the basic theory. "However it happened, it was sloppy. It strikes me as the work of an amateur, with little or no planning."

Ginger's brain whirled. "Do you think it was someone she knew?"

"I'm sure of it. She wouldn't have unlocked that door for just anyone. Do you know if a lot of employees come and go through there?"

She shrugged. "I'm sure there are some, but I don't know how many. Doctors and their staff from the building are probably there from time to time. Delivery people stop by regularly. I don't know how many of those would go inside."

He made a note. "I'll see if I can locate anyone who

makes regular deliveries. There were some drug bottles with pills missing. That seems odd, but it makes me wonder if Martha could have confronted someone about it, and it was a fatal mistake."

As Ginger sat in silent contemplation, he tucked his notebook back in his pocket. "I was curious and did some more research on Tanya Williams, the woman who fell off her balcony," he added when Ginger frowned.

"Oh. I hadn't heard her full name," she said when it came together in her brain. "Did you find anything interesting?"

He shrugged. "It seems she had done stunts like that auction disturbance before. It sounds like she had some kind of grudge toward the owner."

Ginger smirked.

Jon paused, frowning in puzzlement. "What's funny?"

She shook her head. "Nothing, really. I just wondered if yelling about rats might have been the woman's way of calling the man a rat."

He grinned. "Different people have different methods. This woman had been through drug rehab at least twice, but I didn't find anything that says there was foul play involved in her death, or that there's any connection to Martha Peterson's murder."

"So it's a rabbit trail, but an intriguing one," Ginger decided.

Jon's face tautened, a muscle twitching in his right cheek. "Gram's worse."

Her heart ached for him. "Is she your only family?"

"She's all that's close. My parents and granddad are dead."

"Do we need to let hospice know you're ready for them?"

He nodded.

"The nurse they assign to you will serve as your case coordinator."

He nodded, resignation in his sad expression. "Is there any chance you can leave work now? I need to go home and check on Gram, but I need to escort you to your friend's house. I hope you told her you need to stay with her until we're sure you're safe."

"Can you wait long enough for me to call hospice and ask if Elaine Knowles will be assigned as your case coordinator? If she is, I'd be happy to meet her there on her first visit and make introductions. She's a personal friend. I can vouch for the quality of her work."

"I'll be out there when you're ready." He stood and pointed at the reception area.

Ginger made the necessary contact and was told that Elaine would be the RN assigned to the case, and she would be pleased to have Ginger present at her first visit. She would call when she knew her schedule. Ginger disconnected and grabbed her purse. When she entered the front office, Jon stood and opened the door for her. "I called home to check on Gram, and Olive asked me to pick up some Tylenol at a pharmacy on my way home. Do you mind?"

"Of course not. Any particular pharmacy?"

"We have to pass the one where Martha worked. Is that okay?"

"I've been back there since Martha's death," she said, letting him know she could handle the impact of seeing the scene again.

He walked her to her vehicle, waited for her to enter it, and then went to his SUV that was parked three spaces away. When she pulled into the pharmacy parking lot five minutes later, he parked beside her, came to her door, and opened it. "Go inside with me," he said, his tone making it clear he wasn't going to leave her out here alone.

As they approached the entrance, a woman emerged. It was the delivery person Ginger encountered now and then.

The woman raised her hands, palms up. "Everything's delivered safe and sound. I didn't drop a thing." Then her smile disappeared. "I heard you were attacked. Is that true?"

Ginger nodded, surprised at the personal comment. "It is, but I'm fine."

"I'm sorry about your friend. Were you and the pharmacist close?"

"I knew her, but not well. We crossed paths in our work."

"Oh, I see. Well, I'm sorry you lost her. Be careful." The driver headed on to the van parked down the driveway, its rear door visible.

After Jon purchased his Tylenol and they returned to the parking lot, the hairs on the back of Ginger's neck prickled. She had the sensation of being watched.

"What is it?" Jon asked as she glanced around the area.

"I'm being silly," she said, suppressing a shiver.

"I doubt that," was all he said, quickening their pace to her car. "I'll be right on your bumper."

When she arrived at Erin's house, he waited in his vehicle until she was inside.

~

Jon was uneasy about leaving Ginger, but Erin had been at home, and he had to spend any time he could with Gram—while it was possible. Her heart was failing, and the doctor said it couldn't last much longer. All he could do was see that she was looked after and kept comfortable. Olive and the health people would see to her daily needs, but Jon felt so helpless.

He knew his beloved grandparents had put God at the head of their lives and would be in heaven with Him. Their biggest regret had always been their daughter's rebellion during her teenage years and the ultimate tragedy that ended her life.

Jon had struggled with the knowledge of his background after he was old enough to demand to know, and had been told, what happened to his parents. He didn't understand why his mother had wanted to live so recklessly when she had known only love. He had known the love of his grandparents, their teaching of values and morals, with rules to follow. Those rules were fair and designed for his safety and education, but his mother had hated them.

He entered the house and went directly to Gram's room. She looked up from where she lay in the bed, her eyes a little clearer than they had been that morning. "How are you doing?" he asked, darting a look at Olive, who sat in a chair in the corner of the room with her crocheting.

"I'm as good as can be expected," Gram said dryly. She wagged a finger of her left hand at him, while her right arm lay against her side, useless from stroke damage. "Are you up to helping me to the table? I want to eat with you and Olive tonight. Don't know how many chances I'll get to do that, so want to enjoy it while I can."

Olive put her crocheting down and stood. "It's ready. I'll have it on the table in the time it takes you to get her settled and wash your hands."

After the meal, Jon assisted Gram to the bathroom and left her with Olive, who would give her a shower. Gram's right leg dragged, so they had purchased a shower chair. Olive insisted she could handle Gram's slight frame onto and off that, but promised to not do it any more after tonight now that they would have an in-home worker coming each morning.

As he prepared for bed, Jon wrestled with whether to call Ginger. She had sensed something as they were leaving her office. He had, too. It had been a sensation of being watched.

Rather than call, he compromised and sent a text inquiring how she was feeling.

She replied promptly that she was fine.

~

Ginger tossed in the bed, dreaming. The time frame and details were disjointed and fuzzy. She was in her car, driving on a street, when something suddenly penetrated her partial state of awareness. A noise. Her eyes flew open, and she lay there with her heart hammering in her chest, listening.

She glanced up at the alarm clock. It read four-thirty-five.

The sound came again, and then her door opened. She leaned forward, straining to see in the dark. She made out the shadowy form of Erin. "What's wrong?"

"I think we have a prowler," her friend said, coming to the bedside as Ginger swung her legs sideways from beneath the covers. "I didn't want to turn on any light, and I knocked my phone off the bedside table. Can you find yours and call your detective?"

Ginger reached for it on the table beside her. She was able to find Jon's number and dial it.

"Yeah." He sounded groggy.

"We think there's an intruder outside the house."

"I'll head that way soon as I can dress. I'll call Delton and have him meet me." The line went silent.

Erin turned from the window curtain she had been peeking behind. "I saw a shadow go around the corner of the house. I'm going to double check the door locks."

"I'll check windows," Ginger said, grabbing her robe and putting it on as she moved.

They had just completed the rounds, checking each room, when lights flashed behind the living room drapes. Moments later a vehicle pulled into the driveway.

Ginger peeked out and recognized Jon. As he emerged from his SUV and started around the house, a flashlight beaming from his hand, a police cruiser pulled to the curb. The officer she had met earlier, Delton Booker, emerged and headed the opposite direction.

After a tense wait of several minutes, there was a tap at the door. "It's me, Jon."

Ginger opened the door and let him inside. "Did you find anything?"

"It looks like someone tried to jimmy the back door lock

and a window. We heard a car start and roar away somewhere up the street."

Delton stepped through the doorway. "I'll park at the curb until you ladies are ready to go to work. Get a little more sleep before then." He shifted his attention to Jon. "You go back to your grandma and try to get some rest while you're there. You're burning the candle at both ends right now, and you need to conserve some energy for …later."

To his credit, Jon didn't argue.

"Thank you for coming," Ginger said as they headed out the door.

Erin echoed her thanks.

"I'm sorry to put you in this position," Ginger apologized to Erin when the men were gone.

"Don't be," she said firmly. "I know what you're going through. Let me see you through it. Now do what the cop said. Sleep some more."

Ginger gave her a hug. "I'll try."

Once back in bed, she closed her eyes, knowing that a person's subconscious could reveal details people didn't think they remembered. She forced her body to relax, and then concentrated on recalling the dream she had been having before the intruder interrupted. Letting her thoughts drift back to the day of Martha's murder, she recalled driving through traffic toward the medical building that loomed to her right, turning into the parking lot, and entering the building.

She paused. Backed up when an image flashed to the edge of her mind.

As she approached the parking lot, there had been a white van pulling out of it. As they came even and passed one another, a logo had flashed from the side of the van.

Squeezing her eyes tighter, Ginger strained to make out the words on it. Faintly she was able to distinguish one word. It was only one word of the entire logo, but she knew what it meant.

She bolted upright in the bed. "Courier," she nearly shouted into the silent room.

52

Chapter 6

When Jon arrived to escort Ginger to work, she immediately exited her friend's house and walked with purpose to his police vehicle rather than going to her own vehicle. The woman clearly had something on her mind.

He lowered the driver's door window. "Good morning."

She leaned down to eye level. "I remembered something that might explain why I'm being attacked."

He jerked his head toward the passenger seat. "Get in over there and tell me about it."

She rounded the vehicle and scooted inside as he leaned over and pushed the door open. She pulled it shut, faced him, and broke into speech without preamble. "I was having a crazy dream, like a flashback, when Erin woke me about the intruder. After you and Delton checked on our situation and left, I went back to bed—and the dream continued."

He glanced in his rearview mirror and saw that Delton had started to drive away, but stopped, undoubtedly wondering if some new problem had developed. Jon nodded at Ginger for her to continue.

"I was driving down the street, nearing the medical building, the afternoon of Martha's murder," she continued. "It meant nothing at the time, but in the dream, I caught a glimpse of the logo on the side of the van I met. I only distinguished one word, but the word was Courier. It was the pharmaceutical courier van, and it had just pulled out of the medical building parking lot."

His mind was clicking on all cylinders. Did the dots all connect?

"Have you seen video footage of the pharmacy when she was killed?" Ginger asked, interrupting his dot connecting.

He nodded, still wrestling known facts, plus this new one. "I did. It showed Martha seated at the desk when someone suddenly entered the pharmacy from the rear entrance. The person ran across the room, raised a can of spray paint, and painted the face of the surveillance camera."

"Did you recognize the person?"

He shook his head. "He wore a dark coat, gloves, a surgical mask, large sunglasses and a baseball cap. It happened less than ten minutes before you arrived. If you arrange to be late for work, you can go with me right now to watch that footage again."

"I'll call Lillian," she said without hesitation.

While she did that, Jon rang Delton, watching in the rearview mirror as he answered. He quickly explained what Ginger had told him and that they were going to the medical building. "Go on to work, and I'll let you know if we need you."

Delton nodded, waved, and drove away.

Fifteen minutes later Jon and Ginger were back in the small security office of the medical facility, with their surveillance footage on the computer screen. He had spoken to his captain about giving Ginger access to police information, and they had agreed that she could be instrumental in solving the case—and they had to keep her under close guard.

"If you two are okay, I need to take care of something downstairs," the security guard said, moving to the doorway.

"We're fine. Thanks for having this ready for us," Jon

said while shifting the chair to a better position next to Ginger. "Should I let you know when we're ready to leave?"

"That'd be good."

As soon as the guard was gone, they focused on the screen. "Why don't we start the film at about noon of that day," he suggested.

"That sounds good," she agreed. "The few times I recall encountering that particular driver have always been in the afternoon."

It took a couple of hours of viewing, but they eventually spotted the van driver entering the building, and then the pharmacy. Martha met her at the counter.

"Martha seems to be questioning her," Ginger observed, leaning closer.

Jon checked the time stamp. "That was an hour before Martha was murdered. And the conversation does seem intense."

They watched the driver whirl and leave, bypass another customer in the doorway, and then disappear out the front door. Business continued as usual in the pharmacy until five o'clock, at which time Martha locked the door to the lobby and sat at the desk. She was doing paperwork when the intruder entered the room behind her, ran across the floor, and sprayed the camera lens.

"She not only knew the layout of the pharmacy, but the location of the camera," Jon said more to himself than to Ginger, using the feminine pronoun.

"So you think that driver returned to the building an hour after talking to Martha and killed her?" Ginger asked.

"I think it's very possible. I need to find her and ask her some pointed questions."

"I thought her personal conversation—and questions— about my relationship with Martha when you and I met her yesterday were a bit odd. I've encountered her before, but there's never been any personal chit chat."

"She may have been trying to find out if you're onto her.

Do you know her name?"

Ginger shook her head. "We never interacted to the point of introductions."

He turned back to the computer and entered a police database. Within minutes he had a name. "She's Dorothy, known as Dottie, Swanson. Her address is in Nixa, but she's likely at work. I have to go find her."

Jon called the guard to let him know they were done. He met them a minute later at the end of the hallway.

"I'll take you to your office rather than back to Erin's for your vehicle," Jon said once they were inside his SUV. "Will you call me if you need to leave for any reason? I think this gal is our killer, and she's after you because she thinks you can identify her." As she had just done.

Ginger didn't look particularly happy, but she nodded. "Will you let me know if you find her, and how it goes?"

He hesitated, thinking, and decided she deserved the information. "I'm going after her right now, but I plan to take a lunch break and check on Gram after that. I'll call you then."

Before she could answer, her phone rang. She answered and listened. "Just a moment and I'll ask him," she said, facing Jon. "This is your RN. She says she can come get acquainted with your grandmother and complete some paperwork at one o'clock."

He hated the way things were piling up on him, but he had to get this base covered. "Tell her I'll be there."

She relayed the message and disconnected. "Would you prefer to meet her on your own, or would you like me to make introductions?"

"Since you know her, and I've only met her once, I'd like you to be there. I'll pick you up on my way home."

~

"Did you talk to Dottie?" was the first thing out of Ginger's mouth when she slid onto the passenger seat of Jon's SUV at a few minutes after twelve.

He shook his head, starting the engine. "She's working and on the move. And I didn't want to talk to her boss yet, in case he's involved somehow. But after I'm sure Gram's okay, I'll go see him and find out what time she gets off work. Hopefully I can catch her then."

"I called Cheryl to see how she's doing. She's nervous about having to testify against the guy who abducted her and beat up her client."

"If we can get a confession out of him, she may not have to do that."

"Good. You don't think Jimmy Atkins had anything to do with killing Martha, do you?"

He kept his attention on the traffic. "My gut says he's a thief and druggie, but not our killer."

Ginger took that to mean he thought the killer was Dottie. And she agreed.

When they arrived at Jon's house, an older frame structure with a wide front porch, Elaine sat in her car parked at the curb. When she saw them, she exited the vehicle and waited on the sidewalk for them. She carried a laptop in one hand and a satchel in the other.

"You remember Elaine Knowles. She's the RN who will act as your grandmother's case manager and oversee all aspects of her care," Ginger said when they met.

The two shook hands. "Thank you for meeting us like this," Jon said to the nurse, his expression one of solemn resignation.

He accompanied them inside a large room that featured a fireplace at the back wall, a kitchen visible to the right. He took them down a hallway to a bedroom where a frail woman lay in a hospital bed. She opened her eyes as they approached.

"Hi, Gram," Jon said, his tone gentle as he leaned down and brushed a kiss over the pale cheek. "I've brought someone, well two someones, I'd like you to meet. This is Ginger Brewer, director of your home health agency, and the nurse is Elaine Knowles. She's from hospice." He indicated them in turn with a head gesture.

Ginger stepped nearer the bed, smiling. "I'll be working at my office, but Elaine will be coming to see you regularly. You'll be in good hands."

Gram frowned. "Where's Olive?"

Ginger directed a questioning look at Jon.

"She's in the kitchen preparing lunch," he explained. "Ginger and I will go have a bite to eat with her while you and Elaine get acquainted."

As they left the room, Ginger's throat tightened, knowing the grief and loss Jon faced. She silently prayed that God would give him the comfort and strength he needed.

"The hospice nurses work individually, but someone will always be on call if Elaine should for any reason be unavailable," she explained.

~

After a quick lunch, speaking to Gram a bit more, and driving Ginger back to work, Jon wasted no time getting to his desk. He booted his computer and began searching for more information on Dottie Swanson.

His ability to focus on one thing to the point of blocking out everything else helped him cope with times like this. Except that there had never been a time equal to this. Losing his grandmother was getting to him. He needed to be with her. But he had to stop a killer before Ginger could be hurt— or worse. He couldn't let anything happen to her.

Unaccustomed to feeling so helpless, burying himself in work hopefully would keep his mind off those issues.

He logged onto a database and was soon skimming through articles. Dottie had grown up in Arkansas and had parents still living there. There were two more siblings living elsewhere.

He found no police record of any kind, but she did have a concealed carry permit. That set him to theorizing. Could she have had a weapon in her van? Or on her? If so, she could have used the gun butt to hit Martha in the head. It made sense. She wouldn't have wanted to risk the noise of a gunshot being heard in the building.

He tried to envision the scene unfolding. If the blow to the head hadn't knocked Martha completely unconscious, she could have fought and knocked the gun out of the killer's hand. Then the spatula, lying on the counter, could have been grabbed and used to stab her.

Another thing struck him as convenient. If Dottie had returned to the building so soon after that conversation with Martha, the disguise she wore could have been assembled quickly. It wouldn't be surprising for a pharmaceutical delivery van to have surgical masks in it. And a driver would likely keep a pair of sunglasses in a vehicle. A non-uniform coat and a baseball cap could be rounded up in a few minutes. If necessary, she could have made it to her house in north Nixa, a distance of about twenty miles, and back in less than an hour.

He shut down the computer and went to catch Dottie at the end of her shift, which was about four o'clock according to her boss. He had called the man, but had been careful to not raise any alarms in his questions about the shifts of the company's drivers.

A half hour later, he pulled into a parking lot that was about half full and drove to the nearest available empty space at one side of the courier headquarters lot. Easing back in the seat, he scanned the area and waited, it being only ten till four. When a van pulled in at ten after four and the muscular woman emerged, he exited his vehicle and walked quickly toward her. As he approached, she heard his footsteps and swung around to face him.

At first her expression was blank. Then dawning comprehension brought a frown. "I met you with Miss Brewer," she said tentatively. "Are you looking for me?"

"I am. I'm hoping you can shed some light on something for me." He pulled out his badge, flashed it, and returned it to his pocket. "I have some questions. Would you prefer to go inside?"

She didn't look particularly happy. "This will be fine," she said in a tone that implied she might not be too cooperative. "What is it you want to know?"

"I need to know where you were at about five o'clock this past Thursday afternoon."

She shrugged. "I checked in here about this time, like I do every day. Then I went home."

"So why was your van seen leaving the medical building at five after five that day?"

Suddenly her body radiated hostility. "I wouldn't know," she said coldly.

He followed as she stalked away, keeping pace. "You're the person from this company who delivers to that building regularly, and your van was definitely seen leaving it at that time. You can either answer my questions here, or we can discuss it down at police headquarters."

She stopped abruptly and whipped around to face him, glaring. "I don't see how it can be important, but I took off a half hour early that afternoon so I could run an errand. Someone else must have driven my van. Maybe the company had someone take it to the garage. I told them the carburetor has been sounding funny."

"Can you verify where you went after you left your van?"

The question seemed to throw her off balance, but for only a few moments. "I went to see a friend. We discussed a matter, and then I went on home."

"I need that person's name."

She heaved a deep breath and opened her mouth as if to speak sharply. But then she closed it and ran a calculating gaze over him. "Can you be discreet?"

"It depends. I can't conceal evidence, no matter how personal. I just need the facts."

"Oh, all right," she snapped. "His name is Barry

Morgan. He's married."

Uh, oh. It sounded like she was telling him she met a secret lover. He jotted the name in his little notebook. "Where would I find Mr. Morgan?"

Her mouth tightened. "I've never been to his house, but I know where it is." She named an address in a somewhat posh neighborhood.

"Can you give me his phone number?"

She hesitated, but then quoted it.

Jon added the information to his notes. "Thanks. I'll be in touch," he said as she spun on her heel and stalked away.

He drove to Ginger's office, arriving ten minutes before she was due to leave work. Deciding to make use of the time, he remained in his vehicle and dialed home. "How's Gram?" he asked when Olive answered.

"The nurse just left, and she's resting. So don't rush home if you need to do anything."

"I need to make a quick visit to someone. Thanks, Olive."

When he disconnected, he programmed Barry Morgan's address into his GPS. He had just finished when he saw Ginger and her receptionist emerging from the health office.

He exited the vehicle and waited for them to part company before approaching Ginger. "I need to make a visit, and I don't want you driving to your friend's house without an escort," he explained quickly. "It's the opposite direction from the way we need to go, so I need you to ride with me. I'll bring you back to your car. It shouldn't take but a half hour or so. And it'll give us a chance to chat."

Her frown that had formed dissolved at the last statement, as he had hoped. "I'll text Erin and let her know I'll be a little late."

While he started the motor, she sent her text. Then she faced him. "Can you tell me where we're going?"

He nodded, focusing on the dashboard camera while he backed out of the parking space. Once he rolled onto the highway, he explained. "I caught up with Dottie Swanson and questioned her. She claims she left work early that day, and that someone else must have driven her van. When pressed for more details, she claimed she met up with a guy who's married. I want to stop by his house and see if he'll verify that."

It took longer than he had estimated to weave through the streets and stop lights, because traffic was heavy with people heading home after standard office hours. But he eventually pulled up in front of a large home.

"Impressive," Ginger murmured beside him. "Who lives here?"

He saw no reason for secrecy at this point. "Dottie said his name is Barry Morgan."

When he heard a gasp, he killed the motor and swiveled his head around. Ginger's face had blanched, her body tensed.

"Do you know him?"

She nodded. "I dated him once."

Chapter 7

This was an old boyfriend of hers? The thought gave Jon a jolt.

"Once was enough," she added, apparently reading his startled reaction. "We met in a pre-med science class in college, and he asked me out. I was stupid enough to go. He spent the whole evening bragging on himself and his grandiose plans for his future, while putting others down. When he took me home, I told him I wouldn't be going out with him again."

Jon's mouth twitched. "How did he take it?"

She grimaced. "Not well. He informed me that I would end up an old maid because no one would have a cold fish like me." Her expression went solemn. "He may have been right about that, but he's still an arrogant jerk. And it looks as if he's done well as a pharmacist in his father's clinic." She indicated the house with a head motion.

Jon snickered. "I'm sure you've had your chances. You have, haven't you?" he asked when a stricken look crossed her face.

"Yes," she said softly, offering no explanation.

He wanted to ask for details, but he had an interview to conduct. "I'll be right back," he said, opening the door and sliding to the ground.

At the door, he rang the bell and waited for a response. He had reached to ring it again when the door swung open to reveal a mid-thirties guy whose expression said he clearly resented being disturbed. His stare bordered on glacial. Of medium height, he was muscular, his face smooth and too pretty, in Jon's opinion.

"We're not buying anything today," the guy said haughtily and started to close the door.

"And I'm not selling anything," Jon said, whipping out his badge and flashing it.

The guy halted, shooting a furtive glance backward over his shoulder in a way that made Jon think he was checking on his wife—and might have an idea why a cop was on his doorstep. Then he stepped out onto the porch and closed the door behind him. "Okay, what's this about?" he asked snappishly.

Jon cut to the chase. "I need to know if you met with a woman by the name of Dorothy Swanson this past Thursday afternoon between four-thirty and five o'clock."

Mr. Morgan glowered. "If I did, it's my private business."

"When something criminal can be involved, it becomes police business. This woman is implicated in a murder, and she says she was with you at that time. Do you confirm or deny it?"

Pretty Boy stood motionless for several moments. Then he heaved a sound of exasperation. "Does my wife have to know about this?"

John shrugged. "I won't tell her unless it's necessary. But I can't guarantee she won't learn of it from another source."

The glower intensified, but then he said, "Yeah, Dottie came to see me about that time. Now I have a meeting in a few minutes." He turned, entered the house, and shut the door.

Jon returned to the vehicle and scooted behind the

wheel, glad he hadn't needed to go inside that house and leave Ginger out here alone. He finished jotting in his notebook, stuffed it back in his pocket, and started the engine.

"Did he vouch for her?" Ginger asked as he headed back to the main highway.

He nodded. "He wasn't happy about it, but he says she was with him."

He drove back to her car in the mall parking lot, and then stayed right on her bumper to Erin's house. Once she was safely inside, he drove on home.

Olive met him at the door, her expression somber. "She's medicated and resting, but I'm afraid she can't last much longer."

Jon's heart clutched. "I know she's prepared and wants to reunite with Gramps, but it's still hard."

The woman nodded in understanding. "She said she wants to eat with us tonight. It cheers her to be up for even a few minutes."

"Do I have time for a shower before supper?" he asked in an unsteady voice. "I can't tell you how much it means to me the way you've stayed with her all through this."

"That hospice nurse and the home health worker are helping now," she reminded him, clearly uncomfortable at being thanked for doing what she deemed necessary for an old friend.

When Olive wheeled Gram to the table forty-five minutes later, Jon's heart ached at seeing the lines that had been etched in her face by pain and sickness. He bowed his head while Olive said a blessing.

After the meal, of which Gram had eaten only a few bites, she reached across the corner of the table and squeezed his hand. "I love you, Jon. You've been a dear son to me." Then she slumped down in the chair. "I think I need to take my medicine and go back to bed now."

Jon wheeled her to her bedroom and lifted her frail body

onto the bed. "I love you, Gram," he said quietly as she closed her eyes. Then he eased back and quietly left the room.

That night he tossed and turned. Hearing Ginger say that Barry Morgan was a pharmacist had slowly emerged from his grief fogged senses. The man's relationship with another woman, who just happened to deliver pharmaceuticals, stirred a bad feeling in him. He had to dig deeper.

As soon as he had eaten breakfast and spent a few minutes in Gram's room, he obeyed her order and went to work. Once there, he grabbed a cup of coffee from the break room and settled at his desk.

First, he viewed footage of the parking lot of that medical building, but still saw no sign of that particular delivery van. It wasn't surprising, though. With Dottie knowing the layout so well, it made sense that she would have parked somewhere out of range of the surveillance cameras.

Deciding he needed to know more about the delivery system, he started searching. What he read was eye opening. Delivery vans that transported prescription painkillers from warehouses to pharmacies and hospitals were most often driven by independent contractors, and they were targets of an escalating number of thefts. Hitting the right courier could yield thieves a payoff similar to robbing an armored car.

Robberies of these vans were known in the shipping industry as last-mile thefts, because in addition to putting addictive prescription drugs in the hands of criminals, those incidents often took place in public areas, like pharmacy parking lots.

The part he hadn't realized was learning that the van drivers usually received little security training, worked alone, and rarely carried weapons. There were exceptions to that, he reasoned, thinking of his theory regarding the weapon used in this case. This driver had been armed.

"I think I need to talk to Barry Morgan again," he

muttered, shoving his chair back and standing. Something was going on here, but he wasn't sure exactly what.

As he started for the door, his phone rang. It was the captain. "Get in here," the man ordered when Jon answered. "We have a report of a drug courier being robbed."

~

Ginger dropped her head, placing her fingers to one side of her face, her thumb to the other, and massaging her temples. She had spent the morning chasing routine paperwork, anything to keep her too busy to think about anything but her job.

A tap at the door made her look up. Katie was peeking into her office, Cheryl right behind her. Ginger smiled and beckoned for the workers to enter. "You look like gals with something on their minds."

They both took seats facing her. "I wanted to talk to you about Mrs. Haskell," Katie said. "I'm concerned about her. Her doctor changed her prescription, but she's still in pain. Some days are worse than others."

Ginger grabbed a pen and jotted a note. "I'll have her case manager consult with her doctor. What about you, Cheryl?"

"I'm fine," Cheryl said, a hand moving to the crown of her head and rubbing where she had hit the door when she fell after being struck by the thief. "But I'm angry. Mrs. Boswell shouldn't have been hurt like that, or robbed. I wanted to ask if that jerk is going to be put away for good." Her mouth trembled.

"I appreciate your concern, Cheryl. And the detective thinks they might get a confession out of him. If they do, you won't have to testify."

"Well, that's all I wanted. I'm on my way to see Mrs. Boswell."

After both workers left, Ginger called the RN assigned to Mrs. Haskell's case and relayed Katie's concern. The nurse said she would consult with the doctor as soon as possible.

Later in the day, Ginger picked up the phone to make a call, but it rang before she could dial. "Hello."

There was a pause, and then a woman's muffled voice reached her. "This is Lucy. I'm hurt," she said faintly, her voice shaky and uneven. "I came to see you." A pause. "Someone backed into me in your parking lot and took off. I can't walk."

There was the sound of a thud, like the phone had been dropped, and then silence.

Ginger dropped her own phone and raced around her desk to the doorway. "Someone's hurt," she called to Lillian as she ran across the reception area and out the main exit.

She stopped outside the sidewalk, scanned the parking lot, and saw no one hurt.

"Help." The weak sound seemed to come from her right. Ginger ran that way, calling, "Lucy? Lucy!"

Suddenly there was the crack of a gunshot and the twang of a bullet hitting metal. Ginger fell sideways, pain ripping through her thigh.

As she hit the ground, she spotted a figure, crouched low behind a car on the other side of the lot. As a gun rose, aiming at her, Ginger rolled her entire body over. Then she rolled again, passing beneath the frame of the car she had been standing near.

Gritting her teeth against the pain, she lay motionless, listening for movement.

"Ginger! Are you all right?" Lillian's call came from the office doorway.

Afraid to speak and give away her location, she didn't answer. Flattening her body, she peered from beneath the vehicle, straining for sight of anyone, or anything.

Suddenly a motor roared to life. Moments later, two cycle wheels rolled past her ground level eyesight, making Ginger recoil. While trying to decide whether to crawl out of hiding, she heard sirens. Good. Lillian must have called the police.

Carefully, using one hand to cradle her thigh, she reached for the edge of the car frame with the other hand and began to edge her body sideways.

She had just about cleared the car when the sound of footsteps made her look up—way up. A very tall, older gentleman had leaned over to peer down at her through the thickest glasses she could ever remember seeing. His eyes resembled huge shiny marbles. "Are you okay, Ma'am? Can I help you up?"

She lifted a hand, but withdrew it when she saw how bloody it was. Then the sound of a vehicle roaring into the lot and screeching to a halt prevented her from having to say anything.

The next thing she knew, Jon slid to a squatting position at her side. His gaze raked over her in rapid assessment. "An ambulance is on the way."

"How did you get here so fast?" she asked, wincing and peering down at her leg.

"Lillian called the department and asked for me. I wasn't far from here, on my way to do an interview, and detoured here." Concern filled his voice and expression, but his gaze dropped to her leg. Lillian appeared behind him, pale with fright.

"I don't think I was shot directly, but it hurts," she admitted.

"What do you mean?"

"It sounded like the bullet hit metal."

"My bumper has a big dent in it," the tall spectacled man said. "So maybe it ricocheted, and she's not hurt too bad."

"Stay here," Jon ordered when Ginger tried to get to her feet. "The EMTs are here." He backed away to let them get to her.

"Don't worry about anything," Lillian called from the sidewalk where she had been prevented from getting any nearer. "I'll take care of everything."

"Thanks," Ginger responded, watching an EMT wrap a blood pressure cuff around her arm while his partner checked her vitals. "I'm fine," she protested. "It's only a graze."

"But it's a gunshot wound," Jon said from behind them. "It has to be reported, and we want you properly treated. I'll follow the ambulance to the hospital."

"Go ahead and do what you need to do here first," she said, knowing he needed to be part of the investigation.

~

Jon finished his tasks at the parking lot and beat it for the hospital. He believed Ginger's assertion that she was okay, but he had to be sure she was safe, that the shooter hadn't followed the ambulance and waylaid it, or was lurking around the hospital to try again.

He breathed easier when he reached the ER and was told she was being treated, but that he had to wait to see her. It was about ten minutes before a nurse told him he could enter the cubicle where Ginger had been taken.

She sat on the exam table, her bloody slacks that had once been light gray now a splattered mess and slit down the side to expose the wound in the side of her thigh.

He shoved his hands into his pockets to prevent himself from reaching out and brushing back the loose strands of hair that fell across her cheeks. "How are you?"

She winced. "It burns like fire, but it's only a flesh wound. They've given me something for the pain. I'm ready to get out of here."

He studied her face and then glanced at the doctor. "Can she leave?"

"She can," he said, stepping over to the small sink and washing his hands.

"I need to take your statement," Jon informed her. "Let's go find a quiet place."

When she slid off the table, he stepped over beside her. "Lean on me," he instructed, placing an arm behind her waist. She flinched ever so slightly, but let him support her weight as she limped alongside him. He saw her bite her lip against the pain.

The waiting area had several people present, while nurses and orderlies moved in and out doing their jobs. "It'll be more private in my car, and more comfortable."

She nodded, strands of her blondish red, or reddish blond—Gram had called it strawberry blond—hair brushed against his chin.

When they reached the patrol car he had driven here, she hesitated at the door. "I can't sit in there. I'll get it dirty. Bloody. Nasty," she decided, indicating the flapping edges of her severed slacks with a head motion.

"Wait just a minute." He went to the trunk and pulled out an old towel he had tossed in there one day and never bothered to remove.

Once he had spread it over the seat, she let him assist her into the vehicle. "Tell me exactly what happened," he said when he had slid behind the wheel and faced her, pen and pad in hand.

She turned toward him. "A woman called. She said she was Lucy, and that she was hurt. Someone had backed into her in the parking lot. She sounded scared, but it was fake."

"So you were lured outside to help someone you knew, or thought you did, who was in trouble. Whoever it was knows Lucy." One more fact that fit Swanson.

"I ran out the door," she continued, "but I didn't see her. I was standing there, searching the parking lot, when a shot sounded, and my leg was hit by the glancing bullet."

"You never saw anyone?"

She started to shake her head, but stopped. "I saw a figure crouching next to a car across the lot. When I saw a gun raised, I rolled under the car beside me. Then I heard a motor start, and the small wheels of a motorcycle rolled past me."

"The story of the gentleman who owns that car matches

yours. He says it was a black motorcycle with a rider dressed in dark clothes and a knit cap pulled down over the ears. He never saw a face."

"Did his car suffer much damage?"

"The bumper has a dent, but Mr. Danby says he has insurance. He was more concerned about your well-being. Do you have family you could stay with while we investigate?"

"My parents are spending the week visiting my brother in Iowa and won't be home until this weekend. His wife just had a baby. My other brother is in the military and deployed. Erin will injure my other leg if I go anywhere but back to her place. I'll call her, though, and let her know what's happened."

"Speaking of calls, the one supposedly from Lucy came from a burner phone. The bullet from that gunshot must have shattered in a thousand fragments when it ricocheted off that bumper, so we can't identify the type of gun used."

He eyed her injured leg. "Are you sure you can drive your car if I take you back to it?"

"I can," she said without hesitation.

He started the motor rather than argue the point. When he drove up beside her minivan near her office minutes later, she eased to the edge of the seat.

He hurried around to assist her. It bothered him to see her in pain, but he had to admire her tenacious determination to not let anything stop her, no matter how scared she had to be.

When he pulled to the curb at Erin Stuart's house and parked right behind Ginger's vehicle, they were greeted by the sight of Erin coming out the door to meet them.

He exited his vehicle and assisted Ginger to the door, where he surrendered her into Erin's care. He knew she was in good hands here with her friend, but he still hated to leave her. She had been through a lot recently, and he was developing a growing attachment to her.

It was protecting people in cases like this that had drawn him to police work. But he wasn't looking for any personal attachments. They only complicated things. And he already had enough complications.

He had to take care of his grandmother. Deal with all the things the situation entailed.

But he was somehow going to solve this case.

It didn't occur to him until during the night that he had never gotten around to questioning Barry Morgan again.

Chapter 8

Ginger slept soundly until the medication wore off, and then fitfully as she fought pain in her thigh and resisted taking more drugs that could cloud her wits.

"What's cooking in that head of yours?" Erin asked as they sipped coffee at the end of breakfast.

Ginger drained hers and set the cup back down. Then she faced her friend across the table. "I guess I'm just feeling restless, caged. I need to be proactive."

Erin's head tipped to one side, studying her. "Is there something specific you have in mind?"

Ginger tapped an index finger on the tabletop. "I think Barry would lie to provide an alibi for someone if it suited his purpose."

Erin nodded, having been brought up to date before they went to bed the night before. "Are you thinking you'd like to chat with him?"

Ginger shrugged. "Like isn't the right term. But, yeah, I think it might be interesting to see how he would react to having his word challenged."

Erin's mouth moved around in a series of thoughtful twists. "I called my assistant last night and asked her to come in a little early this morning and reschedule my appointments for today. I didn't have anything scheduled that was urgent, only check-ups," she elaborated, clearly not wanting Ginger to feel guilty about her taking the day off to babysit her. "I'll take you wherever you want to go."

Unable to resist, Ginger pushed to her feet. "He should be at the pharmacy within minutes. Maybe we can catch him before he has a rush of customers."

Erin rounded the table to her side. "Lean on me."

Ginger accepted Erin's support because it meant being able to move faster and easier. And it was Erin, who knew Ginger would be there for her if the situation were reversed.

Minutes after leaving the house, Erin pulled into the parking lot of the clinic where Barry ran his father's pharmacy. The sky was overcast, a slight sprinkle dampening the air.

Ginger declined Erin's support this time, needing to stand on her own to face Barry. "Wait for me here," she instructed her friend.

Erin frowned, but didn't argue. "If you need help, call me. Okay?"

"Will do. I have my phone in my pocket." Without taking along the encumbrance of her purse, Ginger walked, limping as little as possible, into the clinic and down the hallway.

Finding that the pharmacy hadn't opened yet, she tapped on the door. Moments later it swung open. Barry stared in startled surprise at her from inside the doorway. Then he peered past her, suspicion clouding his expression. "What are you doing here?"

He was still good looking, and his tone held a smirk, yet Ginger detected an air of curiosity in his demeanor. She stiffened her shoulders. "I came to ask you a question."

His eyes rolled, his face twisting into a disdainful glare. "I'm busy."

"And you lied to the detective," she bluffed boldly as he moved to shut the door.

He halted. "I knew you were a cold fish, but I didn't

know you meddled in police business." He spoke in a superior sneer.

"When I'm being attacked and shot at, it's not meddling. I believe Dottie Swanson is out to harm me, and you're covering for her. If I find evidence to back up that theory, you'll be in trouble up to your arrogant little eyeballs." She turned on the uninjured leg and moved to leave.

"Wait."

She paused, turning back and waiting for his response.

"Are you saying you think Dottie's involved in something bad?" he asked, taking a step toward her. He stopped, arms folded over his chest. "What's going on?"

"I'm not at liberty to share information learned from the police."

He blinked at that and darted a surreptitious glance around the area beyond her, apparently concerned about their conversation being overheard. Indecision flashed across his expression.

"Are you covering for Dottie Swanson?" she asked.

He shrugged. "I guess I could have made a mistake."

"About the time you told the detective you saw her?"

He seemed to wilt a bit, but resentment radiated from his narrowed eyes. "It's possible."

"If that woman happens to be another of your string of conquests, when police catch her, she'll blame anything and everything that you two are involved in onto you."

"Okay," he snapped, darting another furtive look toward the entrance. "She called and said she needed me to say she was with me at that time. When I refused, she said she'd tell my wife about …us," he finished in a whisper.

"Thanks. You can expect to hear from the detective again." Ginger turned and limped away as gracefully as she could manage. She was pleased at having gotten his confession, but wary of the whole situation. She couldn't get out of there fast enough.

Erin met her outside the doorway and tugged Ginger to

her. "Don't talk yet. Let's get you in the car. Then you can tell me what has that wild look on your face."

Ginger concentrated on walking. Once they were both inside the car, she faced Erin. "He admitted he lied. I need to tell Jon about it."

Erin started the motor, and then listened to the details as she drove to Jon's house.

~

"I've already taken care of my funeral arrangements," Gram informed Jon, reaching over to place a hand over his that rested on the arm of the chair where he sat. The home care worker had gone to get groceries, and Olive had gone home for a short break. The nurse was in the next room. "Pastor Richardson has promised to do the service, and Olive will oversee everything else. You just let them do their things and rest in the knowledge that I'll be with your Grandpa Jack and our Heavenly Father."

Jon swallowed hard and fought to keep from looking away. His neck ached because his muscles were so tight. "What will I do without you to order me around and keep me in line?"

She managed a weak smile. "I know someone who might fill that role, if you'll charm her a bit."

How could Gram tease him at this juncture? She was referring to Ginger, who was like him, focused on her job and determined to avoid the complications that relationships entailed.

Movement from behind alerted him to someone's entrance. The RN approached, placed a hand on his shoulder, and gave it a slight squeeze that was a gesture of compassion. And finality.

"Why don't you take a break?" she suggested quietly. "You've been here for hours. She's resting now. I'll stay right here with her and call you if there's any change."

He nodded and pushed to his feet. As he did, he heard the sound of a vehicle arriving outside. At the door, he was surprised to see Ginger and Erin emerging from Erin's vehicle.

He almost grinned as he noticed how 'gingerly' Ginger was attempting to walk without limping, undoubtedly wanting to reassure him that she was okay. He gave her credit for grit. But the somber expression on her face signaled that it wasn't her injury that was on her mind.

He met them on the porch. "What's up?"

"We don't want to keep you from your grandmother," Ginger explained as she paused at the bottom step. "But I have something to tell you."

Jon dashed down and placed an arm behind her waist. "Come on in and tell me about it."

She let him support her weight as she ascended the steps. When they reached the doorway, she looked back to where Erin was returning to her car. "Hey, don't run off and leave me," she called.

"I won't," Erin called back blithely without turning around. "I'll wait for you out here."

Ginger looked over at Jon, her face flushing a bit, probably thinking her friend was giving them privacy in the belief that they were …well, more than mere friends. The idea didn't bother Jon, which was unusual.

He escorted her into the house and to the sofa. Then he sat facing her. "Talk."

"Barry lied," she said bluntly.

He flinched in surprise. "How do you know that?"

"I asked him."

He didn't know whether to scold her or hug her. So he did neither. She shouldn't have been out like that. But it was too late to change anything. "Did you go to his house?"

When she shook her head, he breathed a little easier.

"Erin took me to his pharmacy a little while ago. He wasn't happy to see me," she explained quickly, "but when I, uh, mentioned that he could be in trouble with the police, he admitted that Dottie called him and said she needed an alibi. If he didn't provide it, she would tell his wife about their affair," she finished in a rush.

Now Jon grinned. "So he won't be surprised if an officer shows up with more questions."

Her mouth also twitched. "Will you have someone else do it?"

He nodded, his shoulders sagging as the image of Gram's still form returned to mind. "I'm taking some time off, but I'll report the information and ask the captain to have him questioned. I'll also advise him that Dottie should now be arrested and questioned."

To his surprise, Ginger's arms came around him. When her face pressed against his chest, he cradled her close. A powerful longing caught and held him.

Suddenly she pulled away. A sheen glistened in her eyes. "I'll get out of your way now. I hope there's no trouble with the arrest."

He followed her to the door and watched her make her way down the steps, sensing she didn't want him near enough to observe her crying. It touched him that she would care so much.

When Erin's car had disappeared from sight, he called the captain and was assured that they would bring both Barry and Dottie in for questioning.

He spent the night sitting next to Gram's bed, listening to her breathing become so soft that he wasn't sure there *was* any breath. Early in the morning, she opened her eyes and smiled over at him. "Let the Lord take care of you," she said weakly. Then she closed her eyes and relaxed into the bedding, silent and still.

Jon sat motionless for several long moments, letting the tears flow. Then he watched as the nurse stood from her chair near the doorway and came to the bedside. She checked for a pulse and shook her head.

Later that day, he called the police department and asked for the chief. "Gram's gone," he said when the man's gruff voice came on the line. "The funeral will be Monday. I'll be back to work Tuesday."

"Take whatever time you need," the chief said, genuine sympathy in his voice. "I know she was more than just your grandmother. We'll cover things until you're ready to pick up the reins."

"Getting back to work will be the best way to keep my mind off things, and away from this silent house," he admitted in a moment of absolute truth. "I need to be busy."

"I understand. Some of us will be at the funeral. Since I know you'll be interested, I'll go ahead and tell you that Dorothy Swanson has disappeared."

Jon absorbed that. "She's on the run. I'm sure she's working with the drug thieves, and that robbery of her own van was a hurried diversionary tactic to deflect the investigation in an effort to throw suspicion away from her," he theorized. "It's a cover-up for what's really happening."

"And what is that?" the chief asked.

"I don't know, but after Gram's funeral I'll get busy and find out. There are two things I do know. One, she didn't pull off that fake robbery alone. And, two, it netted them enough drugs to buy a lot of favor with their boss. Or bosses."

~

Ginger and Erin attended church Sunday and followed her parents to their home afterward. During the meal, Ginger told them about her situation in as light a manner as she could.

"I think you should take some vacation time from work and stay here with us," her dad said when she had brought them up to date. He seemed as troubled as her mother, which was not the norm. A school administrator, he had dealt with many police cases over the years. But they had never involved his daughter.

"I need to work," she insisted firmly. "I'll go crazy sitting around wondering how Lillian's handling things." *And how Jon and the police are progressing on the case.*

Keith studied her, reading her resolve, and slowly relented. "How about spending tonight with us, and I'll take you to the funeral you said you want to attend tomorrow. That way Erin can work her normal schedule for the day."

Recognizing a logical compromise, Ginger agreed.

"If she does that," Erin spoke up, "I might run down to my parents and spend the night with them. Ginger has a key to my house, and she can come and go whenever works best for her."

After Erin left, Ginger called her receptionist and explained that she would be taking the next day off to attend the funeral, but promised to return to work Tuesday. Then she followed the example of her parents and took a nap.

The next morning Dad insisted on attending the funeral and sitting in a back pew with her. It wasn't until later, after the graveside service at the cemetery, that Jon turned around and spotted them. When he did, he strode back to where they stood.

"Will you two join us at the church for the meal the women have provided?" he asked as soon as he had been introduced and shaken her dad's hand.

Keith looked at Ginger in question.

She shrugged. "It sounds good."

"See you there," Jon said, heading back to the small group of his grandmother's friends.

An hour later, Jon spoke to Keith again, this time across the meal table. "We don't have our suspect in custody yet. She's dropped out of sight. We need to continue protecting your daughter."

"I'm glad to hear that," Keith said. "How are you doing at protecting yourself? Your emotions, I mean."

Although Ginger read the grief oozing from him, Jon didn't try to avoid the question. "I'm hurting from grief and missing her, but I'll be okay. I know where she is, and that I'll see her again someday."

"Would you mind bringing Ginger home?" Keith asked,

pushing his chair back. "I need to go home, and I figure you two have things you want to talk about."

Ginger rolled her eyes at the less than subtle—and totally unexpected—matchmaking. "I need to stop by my apartment to pack some fresh clothes and supplies."

"That's no problem," Jon assured her.

"If you're sure," she agreed, welcoming the opportunity to speak with him alone. Her heart ached for him.

Soon after her dad was gone, Jon glanced around at where people were drifting away. "I think it's okay for me to leave now."

When Ginger stood, he came around the table and placed a hand on her shoulder. "Thank you for coming. For caring," he added softly against her cheek.

She nodded and let him tug her closer, not caring if the few people still in the building saw them. This was about offering comfort. Forming a friendship. Eyes closing, she leaned into his embrace. Her heart went into a rapid cadence against his ribs.

"Let's go." He placed an arm behind her waist.

They were silent during the drive to her apartment. When he parked in the driveway, they wasted no time going inside the ground floor unit. Once she had her bag freshly packed, she joined him on the sofa where he had waited for her. When he faced her, his gaze was intense. Those dark eyes fringed in long lashes locked on her, causing her stomach to flutter.

She swallowed. "I know your grandmother meant a lot to you. How old were you when you lost your parents, and your grandparents took over the care of you?"

"Eight months."

She caught his hand, compassion overwhelming her. "Did you lose both parents at the same time?"

He nodded.

She slid closer. "What happened? Can you tell me?"

The pain radiating from his eyes seared her heart.

He heaved a deep breath, glanced up at the ceiling, and then back at her. "They fought a lot. One of their fights was so bad that my dad ended up shooting my mom—and then himself."

Her hands tightened on his. "That's horrible."

He drew another deep breath. "No one knows what they fought about. A neighbor heard the shots and called the police. They found me in the kitchen in a high chair."

Her throat tightened. And when his arms came around her, she raised her face to meet his lips as they moved over hers. In spite of the somber circumstances, she couldn't believe how right it felt.

After a long, blissful moment, he pulled away. "I think I should take you to your parents' house now."

She nodded and stood on wobbly legs. As she scooped up her purse, he picked up her packed bag and accompanied her to the door. They stepped out onto the walkway, and she locked the door.

The crack of a gunshot startled them both.

Chapter 9

Jon grabbed Ginger's arm. "Get down!" he ordered, hunkering down and tugging her alongside him. Running, crouched low, they rounded his vehicle to the passenger side, and he yanked the door open. In a flash he slid inside, pulling her after him.

"Shut the door," he barked while maneuvering over the console to get behind the wheel. He jerked the keys from his pocket and jammed one into the ignition as she slammed the door shut.

Glancing in the rearview mirror, he saw no one in the parking lot with a gun, but that didn't mean the shooter wasn't there. He stomped on the gas pedal and backed away from the building, veered forward and peeled out of the lot.

"If Dottie's on the run, why would she risk coming back in the area to shoot at me?" Ginger asked as she twisted around to peer out the rear window.

Jon shook his head, wondering the same thing. "I don't know. Do you see any vehicle that seems to be following us?" He steered around cars and took an off ramp, thankful that traffic was relatively light.

She studied the view a little more before shaking her head. "I don't see any."

He made a sharp right turn onto a side street, and then

took a left, followed by another right. Minutes later, he pulled into a shopping center parking lot and parked at the edge of it where they had a good view of the highway.

"This doesn't feel right," he said, facing Ginger.

She frowned. "What do you mean?"

He tried to analyze what had happened. "There was only one shot, and it doesn't seem that we were followed."

She absorbed his words, and then nodded. "I see what you mean. But why would Dottie, or anyone, go to so much trouble for nothing, except maybe to scare us? It doesn't make sense."

"I know. But whoever did it knows where you live, and probably where you're staying. You need to find another safe place."

"I don't want to go to my parents," she said quickly. "That would jeopardize them."

He tried to think of a better option. And one occurred. He pulled out his phone and dialed. "Are you in your office?" he asked when his pastor answered.

"I am. What can I do for you?" The man spoke pleasantly, sensing nothing alarming.

"Is your safe room available?"

"It is. Do you need it?"

"A friend needs temporary shelter. Can we come there now?"

"Sure. I'll meet you at the door."

When they disconnected, Jon faced Ginger's puzzled expression. "My church has a nice bedroom on the second floor that's furnished with a few necessities. Persons fleeing abuse or other emergency circumstances can sleep there."

This was a terrible situation, but it had certainly catapulted him into storing his grief and moving on with life. He would grieve in private later. Right now he needed to call his superior and report this incident.

After doing so and explaining his intent, Ginger curled her fingers through his. If he wasn't mistaken, he felt her shiver in response. It was with reluctance that he removed his hand and started the engine.

His pastor was standing inside the glass paned doorway when Jon pulled into the church parking lot. He stepped outside as Jon escorted Ginger to the building. Pastor Brice gave them a dimpled smile, his gaze going to Ginger.

"This is Ginger Brewer," Jon introduced her. "Ginger, this is my pastor, Reverend Brice Robbins. He's not such a bad guy when you get to know him. At least his wife and teenage kids like him."

"Come on in," Brice invited, grinning and holding the door for them. "The room is upstairs. I'll take you up there."

They followed him up a flight of stairs that led to a small square landing, and then the stairs veered back another direction. On the second floor, he led them down a hallway lined with rooms on each side and stopped at the third one on the right.

Inside, beige drapes covered a tall narrow window that overlooked the parking lot. The room was Spartan, containing a neatly made bed, a dresser, and a small chifferobe in one corner. It was somewhat musty from not being used recently, but the window could be opened a bit to let in some fresh air.

"There's a bathroom next door," the pastor said, pointing at the east wall.

As a thought struck Jon, he faced Ginger. "I dropped your bag at your apartment door. I'll go get it while you're settling in here."

She grinned slightly. "I guess with no bags, there's nothing to settle."

"I'll give you a key," the pastor said to Jon. "That way you can come and go after I leave. Or do I need to stick around?"

Jon shook his head. "I or another officer will be in the parking lot as long as she's here."

Pastor Brice frowned. "It sounds like you're worried

about her safety."

Jon saw no reason to conceal the situation from the man who was providing them shelter. "Ginger was shot at while leaving her apartment. And it's not the first attempt to harm her."

Brice eyed him in assessment, but didn't ask for further details. Jon appreciated that, not wanting to involve the man in anything dangerous, or share details of an investigation.

"I should call Erin," Ginger interjected suddenly. "She'll be worried when I don't arrive at her house."

"She's spent the last few nights with a friend," Jon explained to Brice. "But we don't want her to go back there and put the friend at risk. And the shooter may have found that location."

"I'll go with you to get the bag." Her declaration was pure intent, not open to debate.

Jon shrugged at Brice and took the key he was handed. "Thanks for everything. I'll bring her back later and see that she's guarded."

It didn't take long to drive back to the apartment building, ask the manager about the bag that was no longer there, and have it returned to them.

They had headed back to Jon's vehicle when his cell phone rang. He didn't recognize the number. "Hello," he said, sliding behind the wheel.

"This is Lucy Thomas at the pharmacy," a woman said, her tone somewhat strained. "I found something in a file cabinet that I ...well, find odd." She sounded genuinely troubled, but professional, and he recognized her voice. He was definitely speaking to the real Lucy.

Jon glanced at the dashboard clock. "I can be there in ten minutes."

"Thank you," she breathed softly.

He put the phone back into his pocket and faced Ginger's questioning expression. He didn't want to take her along on a police matter, but he wasn't about to take her to the church and leave her alone. And she knew Lucy. That might be helpful.

~

"Is something wrong?" Ginger asked, unable to read Jon's expression.

He grimaced, pushing a key into the ignition. "I don't know. That was Lucy. She said she found something odd."

"And you don't think I should go there with you," she charged. "Well, think again, buddy. Somebody involved me in this, and I'm entitled to …"

"You're going," he interrupted, raising a palm.

She heaved an exaggerated sigh of relief. "I'm glad you're a reasonable man."

The reasonable man grinned and started the SUV.

Lucy looked up from whatever she was doing at the far end of the counter when they approached it from the lobby minutes later. Without smiling, she stepped toward them and beckoned toward the doorway.

"Thanks for coming," the pharmacist said as they entered. She closed the door and walked over to the file cabinet at the end of the counter. Then she opened the bottom drawer, extracted a large pill bottle, and returned to where they stood.

"I was looking for something I'd misplaced and found this tucked in the back of that drawer." She pointed over at the cabinet.

Jon frowned. "What troubles you about it, other than that it's out of place?"

Lucy shrugged. "I'm not sure. That's why I didn't call you this morning when I first found it. But the more I've thought about it, the more I've wondered why Martha would have put it there. We're the only two persons who would have reason to be in those files."

Ginger read a mixture of reactions in Lucy, but they added up to one troubled pharmacist. And a memory floated back to her. She addressed Jon. "I'm pretty sure I remember seeing a bottle like that on this counter when we were watching that surveillance footage of Martha talking to that courier."

Lucy's expression underwent a slow transformation, from troubled to one of processing thoughts, and then tentative assessment. Ginger received a quick glance from Jon signaling that they wait for the woman to reach a conclusion she could share.

"Counterfeit drugs are a serious problem," Lucy said, speaking slowly as she picked up the bottle and turned it in her hands.

While she studied the container, continuing to turn it, Ginger's thoughts also revolved. "People can be taking useless, or dangerous, drugs without knowing it."

Lucy nodded, confirming that they were on the same mental track. "Custom package seals, authentication labels, holograms, and security printing are all part of the security system."

"How?" Jon prodded.

The pharmacist tapped a finger rapidly on the bottle. "They help verify that the enclosed drugs are what the packaging says they are."

Ginger dimly recalled reading about a case of that type years ago. "Drug counterfeiters can work with package counterfeiters. Some of them are very sophisticated. Could Martha have noticed a discrepancy in the packaging and questioned that delivery driver about it?" She avoided mention of the driver's name, or the fact that the woman was missing.

"Can you tell me more about the delivery process?" Jon asked.

Lucy nodded. "A courier carrier picks up the bulk drugs at warehouses and delivers them to individual pharmacies and hospitals. Then we inventory and shelve everything. When people come in with prescriptions, we pull bottles like this from the shelves and count out the correct number of doses with one of those." She picked up the spatula lying on the counter. "Then we dispense them."

Jon reached for the bottle.

Lucy clutched it to her. "I'd like to keep this if I may. I want to have these drugs tested."

"Our crime lab can do that," he said.

She loosened her grip. "Do you think we could be dealing with counterfeit drugs?"

"I think it's very possible."

She handed him the bottle. "I suppose this has already been handled too much for you to look for any kind of evidence, like prints. I'm sorry I didn't think of that sooner."

Jon pulled an evidence bag from his hip pocket and held it open for her to drop the bottle into it. "That's understandable. Thank you for calling me."

As they left the building, Ginger had another thought. "One of our workers mentioned a client whose medications weren't being effective, and her doctor prescribing something else. I wonder if nursing homes, private and home care patients, are experiencing much of that."

Jon nodded and opened the passenger door of his SUV. "I think I need to ask area doctors and administrators of nursing homes, hospitals and pharmacies if they're seeing an increase in that sort of thing."

Ginger scooted into the vehicle and glanced at her watch. "It's nearly closing time for most of those places," she said when he was behind the wheel. "And you're not on duty," she added, her mind returning to his loss and her situation.

He started the motor. "It gives me a starting place for when I return to duty in the morning. And, in case you're wondering, keeping busy is therapeutic for me."

~

Jon took Ginger back to the church and saw her to the safe room. Then he went to the parking lot and sat in his SUV, keeping watch for any activity around the building.

The large, paved parking lot surrounded it on two sides, with a much bigger lawn beyond it. Highways ran alongside the north and west sides of the site.

Taking a breath, he called the police chief and updated him to that point.

"I'll send someone to relieve you in an hour," Chief Billings said. "You need to get some rest, especially since you insist on returning to duty in the morning."

An hour later, a patrol car pulled up beside Jon. Officer Deckard waved at him and pointed toward the exit.

The next morning, Jon left his now empty house and returned to the church. "Shall we get breakfast?" he asked when Ginger met him at the door after he called to let her know he had arrived.

He inhaled her by now familiar flowery scent, wondering how she would react if he kissed her again. She had never said a word about the one they had recently shared. He hadn't either. But he had thought about it. A lot. He wanted to kiss her again. But this wasn't the place or time for that.

"I admit I'm hungry," she said, bringing him back to the present. "If we get breakfast burritos in the drive-through, we could eat them at our desks."

So that's what they did.

"Don't leave here," he cautioned when he pulled to the curb at her office. "If you absolutely have to go anywhere, call me."

"Okay," she responded, apparently scared, but determined to stay busy. Like him. Only for different reasons.

After taking the bottle of pills to the lab, Jon spent the morning calling pharmacy, hospital, and nursing home administrators and asking if they were experiencing heavier than usual complaints of medicines being ineffective or stolen. That afternoon he visited several of them—and found it informative.

Some facilities reported normal findings, but others had noted an increase in such problems.

In nursing homes, where residents usually took multiple prescription medications, security measures for controlled substances were not generally as strict. But they, as well as the hospitals and pharmacies, found that drug theft and diversion were most often perpetrated by caregivers, pharmacists, physicians, nurses, and organizations.

Jon was convinced that this case was about drugs, though. But he wasn't certain if it was about outright theft or diversion. At the end of the day he was weary and frustrated. He signed off duty and had started to his vehicle when his phone rang.

It was the lab, so he answered, and was given a report on the bottle of drugs Lucy had given him.

Chapter 10

Ready to leave work when Jon pulled up in front of the office building, Ginger said good-bye to Lillian and hurried out to his vehicle. She noted his grim expression as she slid into the passenger seat.

"Have you gotten bad news?" she asked, buckling her seat belt.

"Puzzling news," he responded briefly. "The lab technician just called, and Max said that bottle Lucy found contains a mixture of placebos and the drug that's supposed to be in it."

Ginger drew a sharp breath at the implication. "Patients can be harmed by not receiving their proper medications. Placebo replacements can go undetected for quite some time, but especially if they're only getting partially replaced."

He nodded. "That's what I was thinking as I drove here. I know there's a problem with health care workers stealing drugs from storage devices and replacing them with water or other substances, but I don't understand how placebos are mixed with high street value painkillers in the same bulk bottles."

He was right. It didn't make sense. Then she remembered something. "One of my workers mentioned a client's meds being ineffective, and her doctor prescribed a different drug. And there was a bottle of pills that only contained half the amount of pills it should have."

"There was an entire shipment found like that," Jon reminded her. "The drug company replaced them, thinking there was an error at the manufacturing plant."

"I suppose drug thieves are most likely to be addicts," she said, unable to grasp a clear picture of what had happened. "But I can't imagine a druggie carrying out anything this sophisticated."

Jon started the motor. "You're right. First thing tomorrow, I'll start contacting more pharmacies and health agencies and asking if they're finding placebos in their shipments."

"And I'll talk to our workers and ask if they're experiencing or hearing of such problems."

"That sounds like a good idea." He pulled out of the parking lot. "Where would you like to go for something to eat?"

Ginger tried to think where would be the safest. "Could we order takeout from a nice place and eat it in the church dining room?" She was resigned to spending another night there.

"That's what I was hoping you would say. Then I could do some research—I have my laptop—while you do whatever you need to do. To pass the time, maybe we could watch a movie online if you like."

"Do you plan to hang around the parking lot again?"

"Delton will relieve me at midnight."

An hour later, after they had eaten, Jon was setting up his computer on a dining table when his phone rang.

"It's Delton," he said, and then answered. He listened for a few moments.

Ginger watched him roll his eyes at whatever was being said to him.

"Midnight is fine. Is that all you called about?" He listened again. "I doubt he has any information near that valuable. He just wants to get out because he's going into withdrawal. But we'll talk to him."

When he ended the call, Ginger resisted asking questions.

He explained anyhow. "He asked if he needs to relieve me earlier than midnight. Then he said Jimmy Atkins, the druggie who beat up and robbed your elderly client, sent word that he wants to make some kind of deal. I figure the chances of him knowing anything very valuable are slim to nothing, but I'll talk to him."

She suspected that the question about being relieved earlier had a teasing dig to it. "Maybe you'll get lucky and he'll come up with a helpful detail, or a name."

It wasn't late, but she was tired. And her leg hurt. She didn't think it was a good idea for her and Jon to be spending too much time together. Alone. She was trying to think of a way to send him away when he looked at his watch.

"I think I should get out there where I can be sure no one is lurking around here," he said, apparently on the same mental track. "Do you need help finding anything, like fresh bandaging for your leg?"

She shook her head. "I have gauze and medicine in my bag. I think I'll take a shower, bandage it, and curl up with a book."

"Would you like me to leave my laptop here with you?"

"No, I think I'm too tired for any more screen time. I had a lot of that at work today."

He leaned over and placed a light kiss on her forehead. "Okay, take it easy. I'll see you in the morning."

~

Jon sat in his vehicle, staring out the window into the dark night, his thoughts on the woman inside the church. She was intelligent and strong, but possessed of a high degree of vulnerability. She intrigued him. He'd known her less than two weeks, but the zing of attraction he had experienced on meeting her had not diminished. She seemed prettier each time he saw her.

In his years of law enforcement, he had never been attracted to a woman involved in a case. He had to be careful, not let Ginger to become a problem—except it was already too late. He had kissed her, which he had no business doing. She needed his clear-headed protection, not an emotionally fuzzy-headed dude with his head in the clouds.

He did a finger thump against his temple. "Focus on the job, dummy. Get the criminals. Keep her safe."

When Delton arrived to relieve him, Jon headed home, fearing he wouldn't be able to sleep. But he was so tired that he conked out almost as soon as his head hit the pillow.

The next morning, he reminded himself to stay focused on the job rather than the petite redhead he picked up and took to her office. He succeeded. Almost.

It was easier to concentrate once he reached his office. He wasted no time before going to see Chief Ward Billings. "This drug case is looking bigger and bigger," he said once seated across the desk from him. "I think we should bring the DEA in on it."

The man's expression became reflective. "I trust your judgment, but I'd like to hear what new developments or details warrant such a move."

Jon went over everything he had learned. "I'm afraid there's a drug manufacturing operation in the area," he concluded.

The man's head moved in a slow nod. "Would you like me to request the agent who worked that undercover operation at the mall back in the summer?"

Jon smiled. "I would. I assume you know he's engaged to the optometrist who became caught up in that mess."

The chief's mouth twitched ever so slightly. "I also know that optometrist and the health care director caught up in this case are close friends. And you're getting to know her quite well."

Jon ignored the personal reference. His chief seemed to

have spies everywhere. "Miles would already be familiar with the area, and his fiancé is planning to marry him at her home church in Ozark before moving to St. Louis with him. Her parents plan to move into a retirement center near them."

"I'll get back to you after I've made contact with him. What are you going to be doing this morning?"

"Well, I'd planned to check back with the pharmacies I've already talked to about any complaints regarding ineffective drugs and see if any of them have discovered placebos in their shipments, but I think I should talk to Jimmy Atkins first. Delton said the guy wants to make some kind of deal."

"Let me know what he has to offer."

Jon left the office and went directly to the jail. When Atkins was brought to the interrogation room, he looked rough. Sitting behind the interview table, he was unshaven, hollow cheeked, and red eyed. His hands, clasped before him, held a tremor. He clearly had been too long without a fix. Maybe he *did* have something to offer.

"What's on your mind, Jimmy?" Jon asked, sliding onto the chair facing the guy.

"Can you get me out of here?" Jimmy pleaded, his gaze darting around the room.

"I don't know. First, let's take care of immediate business. Do you admit you beat up and robbed that poor old lady, and then kidnapped her health care worker and took her car?"

"If I say I did, can I make a deal?"

"I don't know. We have to take it one step at a time. Did you do it?"

"Yeah, I did it," he snapped. "I needed money."

"Okay, now tell me what you know that's so important."

The junkie licked his lips. "I can name a dude who hauls drugs for a shipping company and does some business of his own on the side."

"I'll have to check out your information before we can

talk about any kind of deal. Tell me his name."

Jimmy darted another look at the door, telegraphing that he wanted to bolt. Then he closed his eyes, took a deep breath, and reopened them. "A guy by the name of Duke Harrison sold me some drugs one time. And I saw him and a woman driver together one day. Their routes are in different parts of the city, but they were way out in the county, and they were moving some boxes from one van to the other. I thought they looked suspicious, so I got out of there. Well, my buddy did. I got no driver's license anymore and was hitching a ride with him. I never said anything to him about what I saw."

Jon made a note of Duke Harrison's name. He already knew the woman had to be Dottie Swanson. "I'll do some checking," he said without making any promises.

His cell phone pinged a message as he returned to his office. The chief confirmed that Miles Jarrett had been assigned to work with them and was expected to arrive tomorrow. Good.

Jon reached his desk and booted the computer. He was just set to begin a search on Duke Harrison when his phone rang. "Zalinski," he answered Captain Dickerson, tucking the device between his shoulder and chin while typing Harrison's name into a search engine.

"A white van has been found. It could be the courier vehicle the Swanson woman drives."

Jon grabbed a pen. "Give me the location."

"It's behind a house on North National," the captain said, and then gave him the number. "Owens and I are heading that way."

Jon made tracks for his vehicle and arrived at the address minutes later. Two cruisers were already parked at the curb.

As he parked and walked to the site, it was clear that the courier vehicle had been abandoned, making him wonder if it wasn't the right van. But when he got closer, the logo on the side of it told him it was. The rear door stood wide open, as if someone had unloaded something and split without taking time to shut it.

"The crime lab boys are on the way," Captain Dickerson informed him as he stood scanning the lower income subdivision. Dottie was long gone, either on foot, or had caught a ride with someone else.

As he continued to inspect the area, the forensics team arrived and began examining the van.

"We have a gun," one of them announced.

Jon stepped next to the van where he could view the weapon being extracted from beneath the driver's seat.

"There's also this," the other technician said, pulling out a spatula that matched the one Lucy had shown him at the pharmacy.

"Dottie had a concealed carry permit," Jon recalled aloud, eyeing the gun. "But if she had a weapon with her and used it to attack Mrs. Peterson, she used the butt of it."

"We'll check for DNA, and if we get any, see if it matches the victim," the technician assured him.

Jon nodded, mentally cataloging questions. Dottie couldn't have pulled off that fake robbery of her van alone. Who had helped her? The same person who had given her a ride? Why had she fled after going to so much trouble to fake a robbery? What else was going on? How big was it? And who was behind it all?

The afternoon was about gone by the time he arrived back at the police department. He used what little time was left to call those pharmacies again, this time asking whether they had found placebos in their shipments. None had, but that only convinced him that such discoveries would most likely be noticed by medical caregivers, especially those working in nursing homes and hospitals. The pharmacists only dispensed the drugs. They didn't prescribe meds or provide personal care for patients.

Tired and frustrated, Jon accepted that he was stalled

until those DNA results came through.

As he scooted behind the wheel of his SUV, his phone rang. He almost moaned, but quickly reversed his reaction when he saw that it was Ginger.

"Erin just called me. She said Miles is supposed to be here tomorrow to work with the police, but he's driving on down tonight. She wants to know if you and I will eat with them this evening. She's a good cook."

"Then we should definitely eat with them."

~

"You have to consider that the very people you're asking are among the worst offenders," Miles Jarrett said as Jon finished telling the agent seated across the table from him about contacting pharmacy personnel regarding inefficient drugs and placebo replacements.

Ginger watched the play of emotions that flashed across Jon's face while listening to the conversation.

He grimaced. "I know a lot of pharmacists and pharmacy technicians have lost their licenses for pilfering drugs from pharmacy shelves or from the patients whose prescriptions they filled. And what's worse, pharmacy professionals who are caught for theft represent only a fraction of those who actually steal drugs."

For the first time in days Ginger could relax as conversation flowed in Erin's house. They had a local detective and a DEA agent present, so they should be secure. And the meal had been great. Now they were doubling down on dessert, blueberry cobbler still warm from the oven. Only now had the conversation turned to business.

Jon focused on Ginger. "You can tell your worker that we now have a confession from the guy who abducted her. She won't have to face him in a courtroom."

He returned his attention to Miles. "Hoping for leniency or a reduced charge, Jimmy Atkins gave me a name. I haven't had time to do any research on him yet, though."

"I just thought of something," Erin spoke up suddenly,

looking at Ginger. "My parents are on the lookout for a love seat for the theater. Are you brave enough to try another auction?"

Ginger snickered, the abrupt change of subject unexpected. Then Erin laughed with her.

"What's so funny?" Miles asked, looking from one to the other of them.

"We were ratted out," Ginger said, snickering again. Then she wiped the humor from her expression to explain. "We went to one of those storage shed auctions a few days ago, but we left after a woman created a disturbance."

Both men frowned. "What did she do?" Miles asked.

"Right after the auctioneer started taking bids, we heard a scream. Then this woman began pointing and yelling that there was a rat."

"People started leaving," Erin continued the story. "Then we did, too."

As Ginger's memory kicked in, all semblance of mirth left her. "A couple of days later, I heard on the news that the woman was dead."

Chapter 11

"Tanya Williams apparently had some kind of feud with Bob Caldwell, the owner of those storage units," Jon said, finding it odd that the woman's name would come up again when it was a totally unrelated case. "No evidence of foul play has been found."

Miles frowned. "I didn't see that name in any of the paperwork I read in your drug case. But it does seem familiar."

Jon watched the agent's eyes narrow in thought. Then Miles snapped his fingers.

"I remember now," he said. "That name was on the list of vendors who had booths in the mall flea market when I was working undercover there."

All four of them sat for several moments in silent speculation. For Jon it was more like the clanging of alarm bells inside his head.

"Could she have been selling drugs for Leland?" Erin voiced his thoughts.

Miles nodded. "That's possible."

Leland Zink, owner of the flea market, had been trafficking drugs through market vendors. The vendors involved would make contact with buyers at their booths, and then send them out to the parking lot to make the actual buys. A number of arrests had been made, but there could well have been operators who were not caught.

"If she escaped being detected when others didn't, why was she harassing the owner of a slew of storage units?" Jon asked.

Miles met his gaze. "We'll start looking for answers to that question first thing tomorrow."

"The boss of that operation was a state senator," Ginger spoke up suddenly. "I helped identify him. Do you think there's any chance he could still be behind any kind of operation from prison?"

Jon nodded slowly, as old facts filtered to the surface of his memory. "It's a long shot, but well worth checking. And, if we find a connection," he continued, locking gazes with her and assimilating at warp speed, "there's the possibility that he's trying to exact revenge on you."

"You mean he could somehow be paying someone to come after me?" Her eyes had rounded in fear at the possibility.

"Anything is possible," he granted.

"I'll be contacting the prison warden," Miles said. "Maybe this is all rabbit trail chasing, but it could be a complicated crime web. I'm glad we had this opportunity to gather tonight." He ran his gaze over the small group.

"Why can't Ginger stay here tonight?" Erin asked. "One of you guys could sleep while the other does guard duty, if you still feel that's necessary."

Jon and Miles exchanged looks. "I'm in favor," Miles said with a shrug.

Jon aimed a questioning look at Ginger. She also shrugged. "It's a good thing I have clothes strung all across town," she said lightly. "I can stay anywhere."

Miles addressed Jon. "I'll relieve you at midnight."

"Make it one." That settled, Jon grabbed his jacket and headed out the door.

An hour later, the sound of a vehicle roused him from

his mental fact chasing and theorizing. A dark colored pickup cruised slowly up the street. As it passed the house and rolled out of sight, Jon had the eerie feeling that it had been casing the place. The sight of Miles's vehicle in the driveway and his own SUV at the curb must have been enough of a deterrent to prevent the driver from stopping. At least for now.

When Miles relieved him at one, Jon told him about the suspicious truck. "Whoever it was could come back, but I doubt it," he said after describing the vehicle.

Miles nodded. "No one will get to our women."

Jon started to refute the assumption that Ginger was his woman, but Miles spoke faster.

"It's all right, you know. I have some insight into what I suspect you're fighting. Ginger appears to be a strong woman with a good head on her shoulders."

Jon grinned. "Okay, I admit it. I like her. But I can't let anything distract me from this case. Her safety is important."

"I'll include you both in my prayers. Now get some sleep."

The next morning, Jon and Miles spent time in the chief's office, going over what they knew and didn't know. "I need to start by finding out if the name Jimmy Atkins gave me is important," Jon said at the end of the session.

"And I want to look into that Tanya Williams who conveniently fell off a balcony," Miles said, pushing to his feet.

Working quickly when he was back at his desk, Jon searched for anything that might make a connection between the names that kept popping up in conversations about the case. He read a number of news articles and police reports of interest, but couldn't determine how everything fit.

An hour later, after reading until his eyes hurt, he leaned back in his chair, intrigued by what he had found. He stood and went to the office where Miles had been set up with a computer.

The agent looked up. "Whatcha got?"

Jon dropped onto a chair. "Duke Harrison, the guy whose name was given to me by our small time druggie thug, may be a player. He's the stepson of the businessman who owns that bunch of storage units all over the area."

"You mean the guy Tanya Williams hassled at that auction the girls told us about?"

"The same. Bob Caldwell."

Miles frowned. "Any idea how all this connects?"

"No, but I wonder if Harrison was Swanson's accomplice."

"Run that by me again," Miles said, clearly confused.

"Dottie Swanson is the driver we think killed the pharmacist. She reported that her van was robbed, but I think the robbery was staged in an effort to divert suspicion away from her. In order to carry it out, she needed help. If this Duke Harrison is another driver working with our drug thieves, he could be that accomplice."

"And Swanson has disappeared," Miles muttered, thinking aloud.

"Right. How did you do on Tanya Williams? Find anything interesting?"

"I didn't find any arrest records, but I've been remembering seeing her at the mall, hanging around the booth of the guy who turned out to be the senator's paid assassin. I'm sure she was selling and just didn't get caught. Whatever differences she had with that businessman was between them."

"I wonder if she could have been stashing stuff in his storage sheds, and he found out it was some kind of dirty dealing," Jon speculated. "How about the senator? Did you get anything from the prison warden?"

Miles shook his head, grimacing. "He's not aware of any outside contacts being made, but he assured me he'll check closer into the matter, monitor phone recordings and mail. I think we need to take a close look into Caldwell's business units. That woman's death nags at me."

Jon understood the feeling. "Do you think maybe it wasn't an accident?"

Miles shrugged. "I don't know. I just know there's a bad feeling in my gut."

"What do you want to do?"

He tapped his cheek with an index finger. "I think we're looking at small time thugs here. Someone else is running things and giving the orders. We need to work our way up the chain and determine the identity of that someone. Erin mentioned attending another auction. I think it's a good idea."

Jon nodded. "It might draw attention to us if we all four go together, but I can't risk Ginger being there without protection."

Miles grinned. "We would be right there, but as shoppers."

"I think there are always auctions on Saturday mornings. That's day after tomorrow. I'll call Ginger and see if they want to go then. She can call Erin and let us know if it's a …plan." Miles's grin told him he knew he had almost said date.

Jon made the call, and Ginger said she'd let him know as soon as she talked to Erin. When he disconnected, he started to ask Miles what he thought they should do now, but was interrupted by his phone ringing. He scowled, read the display, and answered. "Zalinski."

He listened to what the captain had to say, his gut sinking. "I'll get right out there," he said when the man finished. Then he faced Miles. "We won't be arresting Dottie Swanson. Her body was found in the woods. She was a lower tier worker who was expendable. The way it looks to me is she apparently got caught by Mrs. Peterson, panicked, and killed the woman. And drawing attention like that was a fatal mistake."

Miles nodded grimly. "Whoever's in charge had her

eliminated. But her mess-ups have put us onto them. We'll nail the scum bags."

"We were right about that last attack on Ginger. Someone, probably the person who killed Dottie, only meant to scare her. Dottie was already dead. They didn't want us to know that yet."

"So your gal's still in danger. Let's go to that crime scene."

~

Ginger stared at Jon, stunned at what he had just told her. "She's dead?"

He nodded, facing her from behind the wheel of his police car. "There's a professional behind all this, whatever it is. So we can't think you're safe just because Dottie's out of the picture now. We'll figure it out, though."

"I know," she agreed, hoping he was right. He had arrived to pick her up after work, looking grim and not as tidy as usual, having been at a crime scene. His no longer crisp pants had mud stains on the knees, and his shoes were mud smeared. His hair was rumpled from the March wind that had been blowing strong most of the day.

"Was she killed?" It had to be what had happened, but she needed it confirmed.

"She was shot, execution style. A couple out hiking spotted her in a ravine. We're reasonably certain she was killed prior to that shooting at your apartment. It appears that she was abducted from her van at the place we found it abandoned, taken to the hills north of the city, killed, and thrown into that ravine."

He must have read the horror she was feeling, because he reached over and gripped her hand in his. What would he think if he knew how much she wanted to slide over and throw herself into his arms? She stared forward, blinking and hoping he wouldn't notice the pulse throbbing in her throat.

"You'll be fine," he said gently. "Miles is still at the scene, and I need to go back there. Another officer will be stationed outside Erin's house." He removed his hand from hers and started the motor.

Somehow Ginger made it through the evening. Erin was already home when Jon delivered her to the door. She followed her regular routine—supper with Erin, some television time, and then feeding the guys the leftovers they had kept warm in the oven after they finally arrived about nine o'clock. They were both visibly exhausted, so the case was not discussed. But to Ginger, it seemed that her world had tilted off its axis.

After a shower, she put a fresh bandage on her leg and downed a couple of painkillers.

Jon went home and Miles went to bed. They had to get some rest before an early start the next day, having assured Ginger and Erin that a local police officer would be on guard all night.

Erin drove Ginger to work the next morning, a patrol car escort close behind them.

Thankfully, her office stayed too busy all day for Ginger to have time to dwell on the most recent developments. But she did have one interesting chat with Lillian right after the woman saw the noon news about Dottie Swanson's body being found. She meant to share it with Jon.

When he arrived to escort her home after work, she scooted into his vehicle beside him. "How did your day go?" she asked when she had her seat belt buckled, this seat becoming altogether too familiar—and looked forward to with too much anticipation.

He glanced over at her, his face somber. "It was long and ugly. While the forensics guys worked the scene yesterday, I pinged Dottie's phone and found it near some vehicle tracks that indicate her body was unloaded there, carried to the edge of the ravine, and dumped. Today I got a search warrant for the phone and located some messages between her and Duke Harrison."

"Did you arrest him?"

"No, we decided to keep him under surveillance and see if he'll lead us to bigger fish. Today we got GPS locations from that phone and spent the day tracking and visiting them. One was the parking lot of one of those big block long lots of storage units. One of Dottie's messages was from a burner phone setting up a meeting at that lot around the time she was killed."

"So you think that's where the actual killing happened?"

He nodded and put the vehicle in motion.

"It was a busy day at the office," she said once they were on the highway, "but I had an interesting chat with Lillian during her lunch break."

He darted a look over at her, and then refocused on the scene ahead. "She's lived here all her life, right?"

"Yep. So she knows a lot of people. After she ate in the break room, she brought me a cup of coffee and made the usual comment about being glad it's Friday. When she asked if I had big plans for the weekend, I told her that Erin and I planned to attend an auction in the morning. I didn't mention you or Miles," she added quickly.

He didn't comment as he veered into another traffic lane, so she continued. "She said she was watching the noon news while she ate, and there was a story about a woman's body being found."

"I had hoped the story wouldn't break so soon," he said, turning into Erin's neighborhood.

"She said they didn't give a name, just that a body had been found and that more information would be announced soon."

"I just made the next of kin notification to her husband, so it'll be on the evening segment—if it hasn't already broken online and through word of mouth."

"Anyhow, Lillian asked if I knew who was killed, and I told her I couldn't talk about it. She's already known about the attacks and my safety escorts, so she picked up immediately that there was a connection. She didn't ask any more questions outright, but she reverted to our earlier conversation about the auction plans and asked which one we planned to attend. When I told her, she looked kind of sick."

"Go on," he urged when she paused.

"I asked her what was wrong, and she said Bob Caldwell is a piece of slime."

Jon parked at the curb and faced her. "Did she tell you why he's slime?"

Ginger nodded. "She said her neighbor's daughter worked for him in his business office, and they had an affair. When his wife found out about it, Caldwell fired the neighbor's daughter, leaving her high and dry, with no job and no employment reference. Lillian understands that the woman made a big mistake, but she still considers Caldwell a snake."

"He does sound like slime, but I don't see how any of that ties to our investigation."

Ginger's mouth tightened. "They say there's no worse enemy than a woman scorned."

He eyed her for several long, thoughtful moments. Then a grin slowly crept its way across his face. "You think that woman might be persuaded to give us inside information about the city councilman's business dealings?"

Her nod kept his smile alive. And when she withdrew a note from her purse and handed it to him, it widened even more. It was the woman's name, address, and phone number.

Chapter 12

"Four units are to be auctioned in this section, and three in the other," Erin said as she and Ginger approached the row of storage sheds. The day, fortunately, was not as windy as the past few had been, and the temperature had risen to the upper sixties. They had exchanged their coats for windbreakers that they wore with comfy jeans and sneakers.

Jon preceded them by a few feet, slightly to their left, and Miles strolled behind them, to their right. Both were near enough to reach them quickly if needed.

They stopped and studied the contents of the first unit where the door was raised to allow such viewing before the opening of bidding.

"This one looks interesting." Ginger pointed at the next open door where the unit contained several pieces of furniture. "Do you see anything there that would be useful to your parents?"

They were walking toward it when suddenly a small tow-headed whirlwind in a red coat came racing across the lot and crashed into Ginger's legs. Shiny dark orbs stared up in shock from the face of a boy Ginger guessed to be about three. A yowl erupted.

Ginger dropped to her knees beside him. "It's okay, young man. We had a little crash, but it's no big deal. You're not hurt, are you?"

"Timmy! Timmy!" A young woman came running up to them, a baby clutched in one arm, and fell to her knees next to the boy. "Why did you run away like that?" Awkwardly she scooped him into her other arm.

Ginger eased to her feet. "No harm was done," she said in a friendly tone, wanting to reassure the young mother. "He was being a little boy."

"Hi, Melissa. Will you let me hold the baby?" Erin stepped forward, arms outreached.

The young woman's head swiveled around, and she stared upward from her squatted position for a moment. "Dr. Stuart," she said in surprised recognition. "Thank you." She handed Erin the baby and tugged the sobbing boy to his feet. "Come on, Timmy. I have to go get Cassie's stroller."

"We'll watch them both while you get it," Ginger said, reaching for the little boy's hand.

"Thank you," the young mother said, placing the child's hand in Ginger's. She whirled and ran back the way she had come.

Ginger held onto the boy's hand when he tried to pull away and follow his mother. "She'll be right back, Timmy. Why don't we chat while we wait for her? How old are you?"

The kid glared at her, as if his age was none of her business. But then he glanced after his mother and raised a hand, the thumb holding the index finger down so the other three fingers were left pointing upright.

"That's how old I guessed you to be. What do you want to be when you grow up?"

He squinted, considering. Then he grinned and said, "Big."

Ginger and Erin were both snickering when his mother returned. "Thank you for being so gracious," she said, pushing a stroller to a halt. She took the baby from Erin and stooped to place the pink clad child in the seat. Then she stood upright and faced them again. "I don't usually bring the kids to these sales, but my mother couldn't keep them this morning."

"Do you attend many of them?" Ginger asked, recognizing what might be an opportunity to ask questions.

Melissa nodded. "I buy interesting furniture pieces, mostly wooden. Then I rehab them and let my parents resell them in their thrift store."

"This is something new for us," Ginger said, while noting Jon's presence a few feet in front of them. "We attended one a couple of weeks ago. It was an interesting experience."

Melissa's brow creased. "Oh? Where was it?"

Ginger named the location.

Melissa grinned. "I was there. So I know you're referring to the scene that woman created."

Ginger nodded. "We didn't stick around and bid on anything. Did you?"

Melissa grinned. "I did. There was a unit that had some things in it that looked interesting."

"Did you get them?" Erin asked.

"Yes. And I found some treasures in the mess."

"What about the disruption? Did that get settled?"

Melissa frowned. "Mr. Caldwell escorted the woman out of the unit."

"You never saw them after that?"

"No. Well, not exactly," she amended. "My dad came with his trailer to get my stuff, and when we were loading, I heard their voices from behind the building. They were arguing and probably didn't realize how loud they were getting. I heard the woman yell something about him—I guess she meant the owner—and the fiddler, or the fiddle, or something like that."

It didn't make sense to Ginger. "It sounds like there must have been a fiddle, or at least something personal, in a unit that she wanted."

Melissa clutched at Timmy's hand again when he tried

to jerk free of her grasp, her expression turning thoughtful. "These storage auctions are held when people fail to pay their rent. But if they do it without the person's knowledge, it falls under conversion, the illegal taking of someone's personal property without their consent. Maybe something like that happened."

"I'm sure renters of these sheds have to be sent notifications before their possessions can be sold," Erin said, scanning the block of units. "Maybe she was claiming she hadn't been notified, or that she had mitigating circumstances. Oh, there's no use speculating," she decided.

"I heard the woman had a fatal fall over her balcony," Ginger said. "Did you know that?"

Melissa shook her head, dismay clouding her expression. "I didn't know. I had no idea the poor woman was dead."

"Ladies and gentlemen," the auctioneer announced over the loudspeaker. "It's time to begin. Do you all have your registration cards?"

"I need to get back over there." Melissa pointed at the next open unit door. "That's the one I want to buy. It was nice to meet you."

Ginger and Erin watched her turn and hurry away, pushing the stroller and clasping one of Timmy's hands onto the handle of it.

"He thinks he's pushing the baby," Erin observed, a touch of humor in her tone. "She's a good mother. Let's see how the bidding goes on this unit."

~

Jon had moved to a position that provided a peripheral view of Ginger and Erin while they chatted with the young mother. He could only hear snatches of the conversation, but the encounter struck him as providential. He heard enough to know that their previous auction experience had been discussed.

When Erin bid on, and subsequently bought, the

contents of the unit, he shot a raised brow look over at Miles, whose expression was similar. They obviously agreed that pulling that trailer behind his truck had been a good move.

After Erin had paid for her purchase, the four of them met in the parking lot, where Jon and Miles insisted the women stay in Erin's vehicle together while he and Miles loaded the loot.

"I think Caldwell is involved in the drug operation. I just don't know how," Miles said an hour later, speaking to the group sitting around Erin's table during a late lunch of burgers they had picked up on the way to her house. They still had to haul the loot to her parents in Ozark.

Jon nodded. "I'm pretty sure I spotted Duke Harrison in the parking lot at one point. I'd love to talk to both of them, but I don't think we should do that yet."

"You're right. We need to keep them under surveillance and see if we can track them to some kind of proof, like their base of operations. At this point, I think Caldwell is looking good for the ringleader."

"We need to be careful and not tip them that we're onto them," Jon added. "If that happened, they could do something deadly. What I *would* like to do is talk to the woman Caldwell used and spurned."

"And I," Miles said, pushing his chair back, "need to contact some more pharmacists privately about having their bulk containers of drugs tested."

Erin looked over at Ginger. "I need to go grocery shopping. Would you like to go with me?"

Ginger shook her head. "I want to go with Jon."

Jon read determination in her eyes and the set of her chin. He shouldn't take her. But she couldn't be left here alone. And Erin wasn't her bodyguard. She was his responsibility.

"All right, let's go." He scooped debris from the table and took it to the trash can.

When they arrived at the address the receptionist had

given Ginger, Jon rather enjoyed her presence beside him. He had decided that having another woman present might make the interviewee more comfortable, and hopefully more forthcoming.

He rang the doorbell, hoping the woman was home. The door opened enough for a feminine face to peer past the security chain. He held up his badge. "I'm Detective Zalinski, and if you're Megan Lathrop, I'd like to ask you a few questions. May we come inside?"

There was a hesitation, but then the chain was pulled back and the door opened wider. "I'm Megan, but I haven't been involved in anything that should interest the police," the tall, blond woman said. Jon already knew from research that she was thirty-four and divorced, the mother of two junior high boys who lived with her and spent most weekends with their dad.

"This is Ginger Brewer," he introduced once they were in the living room. It wasn't the most tidy, but had what Gram would have called a lived-in look. "May we be seated?"

Megan shrugged. "Sure."

He waited until she had perched on the sofa and he was facing her from an easy chair to begin. "My intent is not to make you uncomfortable, but I'd like to ask what you can tell me about a man you used to work for."

The woman emitted a hiss of breath and slumped back onto the sofa cushion. "I knew this was bound to happen someday. What's he done now?" She returned to an upright position. "You are talking about Bob Caldwell, aren't you?"

"Yes, Ma'am. We understand that you had a close relationship with him."

"It was so stupid," she practically moaned, rubbing her hands over her face. "I was still reeling from the shock of being left for another woman, and Bob was smooth talking and good looking. And my boss. I fell for his line."

Jon had heard too many such stories to deny how often

it happened. He needed to know more, but hated having to ask. "He was married, wasn't he?"

She nodded, her mouth forming a grim line. "He said his wife didn't care what he did, and even implied that she played around as well. I guess she was more tolerant than his first wife."

A quick glance from Ginger made Jon think the idea of another possible source of information could exist. "What's the first wife's name? Do you know where I could find her?"

She splayed her hand on the cushion beside her, swaying slightly. "Her name was Beverly. I only know that because I looked it up. I have no idea where you can find her."

This was a rabbit trail, but Jon felt compelled to follow it. "Does that mean you tried?"

She nodded jerkily. "I was curious. One day I had heard another employee say something about a first wife. This was while I was still working there and …seeing him. I asked a friend what she knew about her, and she said Bob's story was that Beverly cheated on him, divorced him, and left town with her lover. There were no children, and Bob's story was believed."

"But you don't believe it?"

"I don't know what I believe," she said weakly, reaching over and yanking a tissue from the box on the end table. She promptly began to shred it with her fingers. "I didn't think any more about it until …"

He waited, noting Ginger's silent absorption.

"I don't know what I believe," the woman repeated haltingly, as if unsure how to phrase whatever she meant to say. "The second wife wasn't as uncaring as he said. One day she walked into the office and saw him kiss me. She was furious and demanded he get rid of me. So he fired me. And he told me that if I ever said or did anything to cause him trouble, he'd sue me for embezzlement. So I've kept quiet," she said after another long pause, "even though I never did anything wrong. But I couldn't stop wondering about the first wife, if she had any kind of threats like that. But I can't find any trace of her."

Jon nodded, making a mental note to do some checking of his own. "How successful is Caldwell's business? Is there any reason he might have used that term embezzlement?"

Megan frowned in a way that made him think it was a new concept to her. Then she slowly shook her head. "It produces a steady income flow, and I never saw anything that led me to think he was doing anything wrong. He made a little extra from his city councilman position, but not a lot. But he spent a lot," she added hesitantly, stressing the word lot. "He has step kids living it up in college, or he did then. And he has expensive tastes. So does his newest wife, if her car and clothes are any indication."

Jon considered how to ask his final question—and decided straight out was the only option. "Is it possible that your former boss could be involved in any kind of drug operation?"

The woman's eyes went round as saucers. "I don't know," she said after several moments. "I never saw anything that would even hint at such a thing."

"Okay, thank you for talking so openly with me." He stood and turned to leave.

A sharp intake of breath behind him made him turn back around. The look on the woman's face held a mixture of bewilderment and shock. A hand covered her mouth.

"You remembered something?" He sank back onto the chair.

She nodded. "It may not mean a thing, probably doesn't," she said slowly, her eyes practically rolling in agitated thought. "One day I overheard part of a phone conversation. I don't know who Bob was talking to, but he mentioned something about his overseas account. His back was to me, so he didn't know I had entered the room. I stepped back and left, and never thought any more about it.

Do you think it could be important?"

"I don't know, but I'm glad you remembered and shared it. Thank you again."

He and Ginger were both silent as they returned to his vehicle. When he was behind the wheel, he pulled out his notebook and hurriedly jotted some notes. He hadn't done that inside, hoping the woman would be more forthcoming if he wasn't sitting there making notes like a stenographer.

"What now?" Ginger asked when he finished. "Do you plan to look for that first wife?"

He nodded. "Delton's been working on a couple of cold cases lately and seems to like the work. I think this is something right up his alley."

Before he could say more, his phone rang. It was Miles. "Zalinski."

He listened to what the agent had to say, disconnected, and faced Ginger. "That was your friend's fiancé. He said more pharmacists and hospitals have found bulk containers with half the number of genuine drugs they're supposed to contain, and a matching number of placebos."

Chapter 13

"This is a very sophisticated operation," Ginger said when she and Jon were seated in his SUV. His rugged profile beside her caused a jelly jiggle in her mid-section. "Drugs are being diverted, half of them replaced with placebos, and then repackaged and delivered. But I can't figure out how it's all done."

"We'll figure it out," he said, starting to turn the key. "We know a lot more than we did."

She tilted her head in thought. "But there's too much we don't know. We think Dottie killed Martha, but there's not enough solid proof yet. We know another driver is involved, but is he the only one? And what about the death of Tanya Williams? Was it an accident—or murder?"

"We know she was a vendor at the mall," Jon continued when she paused. "My gut says she was selling drugs, and her harassment of Caldwell suggests he's probably involved."

Her mind shifted gears. "Martha's ex and her son were both cleared, but I wonder if either of them knows anything about Martha's suspicions or confrontation with Dottie."

Silent for a moment, his brow crinkled. Then his head began a slow nod. "You're right. Maybe she said something to one of them. It might also be worth asking if they know

Williams or Caldwell, or whether Martha ever mentioned them. Let's go see them."

"You mean right now?"

"Sure. I don't remember the exact address, but I know the street, and I'll recognize the house when I see it." Decision made, he started the motor and rolled onto the highway.

Ginger tried to relax as he drove, but tension grew until her neck and shoulders ached. When he exited the highway onto a residential street, she leaned forward. When he pulled to the curb in front of a white frame house with brown trim, they each opened their car door. She bit her lip as they approached the front porch.

Jon rang the doorbell. Moments later the door opened.

"It's you again?" The gangly, bushy headed man's bark was not friendly. "What do you want now?"

"We'd like to ask a few more questions, hoping you can remember something that will help us identify whatever the mother of your children was apparently investigating."

"What's this about?" The teenage son appeared at his dad's shoulder.

"It's that cop about your mom again," the dad explained to the boy. Scowling, he backed up and opened the door wider. "They want to ask more questions."

The boy glared, his mouth tight, but he refrained from speaking.

"We won't take a lot of your time," Jon said as they stepped into the living room. Across the room, the younger sister peeked around a doorsill, and then instantly disappeared. He focused on the boy. "Do you recall your mother mentioning any trouble at work?"

The young man frowned, more puzzled than belligerent now. "You're not checking on us again, are you?"

"We know you've been cleared," Jon repeated for the young man. "We just want to nail your mother's killer and hoped you could help."

He seemed to relax a bit. "She didn't talk about her work much. I guess it was confidential," he said slowly. "But …" He paused, as if recalling something.

They waited.

"Now that I think about it," he continued, "that last morning she did seem unusually tense, almost scared."

"Did she say anything at all?" Ginger piped up, wanting desperately for him to remember.

The boy frowned in concentration for several moments. "She made a crack about some labels bothering her, but I don't know if she was referring to something at work, or just something around the house."

Jon placed a hand on Ginger's arm in a signal to leave. But as they turned, she hesitated and faced the two again. "I have one more question. Do either of you ever remember hearing Martha mention the name Tanya Williams?"

Both males frowned.

"I don't," the boy said.

"I remember hearing the name, but I don't think it was from Martha," the adult said. "She and I didn't talk a lot anymore."

"You probably heard it on the news," Ginger said, disappointed. "She fell over her balcony and died."

The ex's eyes narrowed. "That's right. And then I heard someone at work mention it later. I can't remember which guy said it, but he kind of snorted and said he guessed they finally caught up to her. I don't know what he meant, and I was too busy to stick around and listen to any more of the gossip."

"Thank you for your cooperation," she said, smiling.

Jon repeated the thanks, and they left.

"That seems to confirm that the dead lady was involved in the drug business," Ginger said as they returned to Jon's vehicle.

"And Martha's concern about labels indicates she had noticed something about the packaging of those pills," Jon added, pulling the passenger door open for her.

He had just started the motor when the loud crack of a gunshot startled them.

"Get down," he ordered, shoving the SUV in gear and peeling away from the curb.

"I don't see anyone," Ginger said, easing up to peer through the window.

"I don't either. Someone is probably perched in a tree or on a roof with a rifle. And someone in a house, most likely the one we just left, is probably calling 911." He drove to the end of the street and veered left onto the main thoroughfare. When no more shots were heard, he surmised that he had been right about a stationary shooter.

"I think we're clear now," he said five minutes later, still heading south. "I'm afraid we've been tracked. We need to switch vehicles. Let's go get yours."

"And go where?" she asked a bit stridently, still shaken.

He glanced over at her, frowning. "We have to find a safe place to hide while I figure out who's after us."

She frowned, but nodded. "I can't go back to Erin's and put her in any more danger. And I don't want to go back to the church. They don't need a stowaway, especially when they have services in the morning. And I'm afraid you're a target now also."

Jon acknowledged her deduction with a shrug. "If someone thinks he can scare me off the investigation, he's wrong."

"This operation must be bigger than we thought, for them to kill anyone who gets in their way." A chill crept through her. She was caught up in something with no end. They couldn't walk away from it and still be killed. They had to see it through. "I trust your judgment," she said, meaning it.

~

Jon gave her a curt nod, glad she had come around to that. "I think we both need to arrange some time off work.

It's no longer safe for you at your office. Then we need to replace our phones and go somewhere safe. I think I know a place that's secluded enough for that. It's about twenty miles from here. Call whoever can cover for you, and I'll do the same when I get to your apartment. Then I'll call in a report while you grab some clothes, and we'll stop at a grocery store for some provisions on our way out of town."

He listened while driving as she called her receptionist. "Lillian says she can handle the office until I can get back to work. She also gave orders for us to be careful and promised to speak to no one but the police if asked about us," she said after disconnecting.

He pulled to the curb and parked beside her minivan near her apartment. Next, he called his chief and gave him a quick summary of their situation, promising to keep in touch as he could. Then he escorted Ginger inside. Once there, he called his pastor and asked where he could find a key to the staff building of the church camp. By the time he finished, Ginger had packed an overnight bag and grabbed some blankets from the closet.

Minutes later, they entered an electronics shop and purchased phones. Then he drove down the road to a grocery store. As he drove Ginger's car out of the lot minutes later, a rumble from his stomach reminded him that they needed sustenance now. So he pulled into a fast food drive-thru for burgers and fries that they ate as they traveled. The city of Springfield was mainly flat, but rolling hills and cliffs surrounded the south, east, and north sections.

As they finished eating and traffic thinned, he drove a little faster, anxious to reach their destination. "You feel better?" he asked as Ginger stuffed their wrappers in the fast-food sack.

She inhaled deeply. "My stomach does, but I admit I'm still scared."

"That's not all bad," he said. "Being a little scared will keep you alert. Do you remember where to turn off to the church camp?"

"I think so, if it's the one out this way that several of our local churches use. Is that where we're going?"

He nodded. "My pastor said there's a key to the staff cabin hidden in a metal box under the big root of a tree behind the building."

She pointed ahead. "I believe that's the road we want."

He turned onto it and rolled down a narrow gravel road lined with towering trees and overgrown foliage that hadn't turned green yet.

Soon they entered an open area with two big barracks style buildings in the center of the grounds. He knew one had a kitchen and dining hall upstairs, with a huge open basement below where worship services were held for the groups of young campers who occupied the camp throughout the summer. The other building was where the nurse, cook, camp pastor and other non-counselor workers were housed. There were cabins in wooded areas to the south for male campers, and cabins for the girls to the north. Beyond them to the west were a swimming pool, and an open recreation field not far away.

"The pastor said we can get into the kitchen if we want. There are keys to that building as well as the staff barracks hidden where he told me to look. I forgot to ask if the electricity is turned off for the winter."

It was a relief to find that there was power once they were inside the staff barracks. He set her bag on the floor. "You can stay here, and I'll sleep in the other building," he decided, now that he knew Ginger was safe. That would be close enough for him to get to her if, heaven forbid, anyone came prowling around. "Are you all right?"

She nodded, not meeting his gaze. "I'm fine."

To him she seemed a bit forlorn. He fought the urge to take her in his arms and comfort her. She hadn't mentioned their kiss, but he hadn't either. It simply hovered invisibly between them, the elephant in the room. This wasn't a good time or place to repeat it. She seemed to radiate that same sentiment. Their safety—and the case—were paramount.

The rooms were cool, but not so much that they needed heat while sleeping. He watched Ginger toss the blankets she carried onto a chair.

"I don't think I'm ready to sleep yet," he said, visually scanning the room that held nothing more than that chair and a bench seat. "Why don't I bring in that bag of groceries before hitting the hay?"

"That sounds good," she agreed, standing before the window that showed it had turned nearly dark outside.

~

When Jon turned and exited, Ginger took two of the blankets to the first room on the right down the hallway. She spread one over the cot and laid the other across the foot of the bed. Then she went to the bathroom in the rear of the building and washed her hands.

Back in the front room, she plopped onto the bench seat and leaned back against the wall. What a trip this had been. She liked that big hunk of a detective-bodyguard way too much. Not smart. Personal involvement was wrong. But she had to stick with him until they found some closure on Martha's death.

Her self-admonishment was interrupted by Jon's return.

He set the large bag in the floor and peered into it. He pulled two bottles of water from it and handed one to her before sitting in the chair beside her.

As she sipped and swallowed, her brow puckered in thought. "This is a crazy situation. You shouldn't be stuck looking after me."

He waved a palm in dismissal. "Don't feel that way. It's become more than just my job. I want to know you're safe. In fact, I'd like to know more about you. You know my history. What made you the caring person you are?"

She grimaced. "Don't make me out to be something I'm not. I have my issues."

"I know you don't have the love for God I would have expected. Why is that?"

She drew a harsh breath and placed the bottle on the floor. Maybe it was time to share it, let him see how shallow she really was. "I was engaged to be married. Two weeks before the wedding, a drunk driver crashed into Aaron's truck, and he was killed. The driver walked away with only minor injuries."

"And you're angry with God—and that man," he murmured, placing a hand over hers. "I can only imagine how hard it must have been. I don't understand why things happen the way they do, but I know God's there for you. If you'll seek Him, He'll give you peace."

She considered his words. Maybe he was right. She stared at his fingers that enclosed hers, feeling an unexpected—or sought—connection to him.

She pulled in a deep breath and forced a smile to her mouth. "I'm gradually gaining a new perspective, but there are still times when I question why God took Aaron away from me."

"I believe He has a reason, but it just hasn't been revealed yet." His voice had become husky. "I do know that God loves you."

"What about you? I assume you've never been married." The words slipped out without forethought.

"No," he said, smiling. "I considered it once, but it didn't work out. My job requires all my energy and attention, keeps me too busy."

"You don't think you could find a balance?"

Their gazes locked, the air shimmering with a charge of awareness.

"I haven't thought so," he said quietly, moving closer. When he lifted her chin with his fingers and bent his head toward hers, she swayed against him. Then he kissed her— tentatively at first, and then with gentle tenderness. Her heart hammered with utter joy as his lips moved over hers.

After several wonderful moments, he pulled away. "I think I'll really have trouble going to sleep now, but it's time to give it a try. I'll take the grub to the kitchen."

Ginger watched him pick up the groceries and blankets and walk out the door—leaving her wrestling with her tangled feelings toward him.

Chapter 14

Jon dozed, but roused every hour or two to look outside and be sure everything was secure. Then thoughts of Ginger would prevent him from going right back to sleep.

He ached for her. She had obviously loved her fiancé very much and had not yet recovered from the loss. It explained her loss of communication with God. She blamed Him.

He knew God could, and would, heal her. But she needed to reach out to Him. All he, Jon, could do was pray that would happen.

He fell asleep praying and woke again as the sun was peeking over the horizon. He slid off the cot he had found in the little room behind the kitchen and put some water on to boil for coffee, thankful for electricity, lights and the stove.

Jon rubbed a hand across his rough chin and jaw, wishing he had a razor. He settled for washing up at the sink in the Spartan little bathroom.

He was rummaging in the refrigerator when the creak of a floorboard made him look over his shoulder. Ginger stood just inside the doorway. "I was going to heat these frozen omelet meals," he said, taking them from the freezer and facing her with them. "It's not fancy, but it's sustenance."

She produced a weak grin. "We agreed on that when we

bought them. I'll fix the coffee if you want. I assume that's why you're boiling water."

"Have at it. I'm in need of caffeine."

When the food was hot, he put it on the kitchen work table between the steaming mugs of coffee each side of the table. Then he bowed his head and thanked God for the food and shelter.

They didn't talk much while eating. "I'm sorry we can't attend church today," he said when they finished. "Would you like to go for a walk around the grounds and enjoy God's creation?"

"That sounds refreshing, and I need the exercise," she agreed.

The rest of the day passed in a blur. They hiked in the woods that surrounded the campground. At noon they cooked and ate spaghetti.

"I need to make a couple of phone calls," he told Ginger after tidying the kitchen. "How about you?"

She nodded. "I need to contact my parents and let them know I'm okay. Since I didn't meet them for church, they'll worry about me."

They powered up their new phones. While she talked to her parents, he called Chief Billings and brought him up to date.

"If I hear anything helpful, I'll call this number," the chief said when Jon finished.

"It'll probably be turned off, but I'll check it periodically. I'm not sure when I can get to the office. If we're not disturbed tonight, I may try to come in sometime tomorrow. We're driving Ginger's vehicle."

"Be safe," the man said gruffly before disconnecting.

Jon saw Ginger turn off her phone, but he dialed his again, this time Delton's number.

"What's up with the new phone number?" his colleague asked when Jon identified himself.

He started explaining. "I have something I'd like you to

look into," he said when finished. "You've been working on cold cases. Have you by chance run across one on a woman by the name of Beverly Caldwell? The name could have changed, but she's the first wife of Bob Caldwell. They divorced, and so far as I can determine, she's not been seen or heard from in the six or seven years since."

"That name sounds familiar," Delton said. "But I don't recall any details. I'll get on it right away. Is there anything I can do for you right now?

"Just keep your ears and eyes open and contact me at this number if you run across anything I need to know."

"Will do."

The rest of the afternoon was a peaceful interlude that included a nap and exploring the grounds, but to Jon it felt like the calm before a storm.

"We'd better get all the rest we can," he cautioned after another simple meal from their supplies. Rather than risk the temptation of another kiss, he put the last of the dishes away and faced Ginger. "I guess we should turn in now and leave early in the morning."

She nodded, recognizing the dismissal. If the way she moved closer to him and abruptly stepped back was any indication, she understood. "Good night," she said hastily before turning and shooting out the door. He watched until she disappeared inside the staff cabin just up the hill.

Jon didn't sleep soundly again that night and slid from the cot at the crack of dawn. Minutes later, Ginger joined him in the kitchen, looking more chipper than he felt. She also had the advantage of a fresh change of clothes.

After bowls of cereal, they tidied the areas where they had slept and eaten, locked everything up tight, and headed out to the highway.

~

As they traveled down the interstate, a cluster of storage units to their right caught Ginger's attention. As they rolled past them, memories of the first auction she and Erin had attended came to mind. She visualized the scene, and then the disturbance, followed by the owner's appearance.

Caldwell had acted business-like, but irritation had gleamed from his deep-set eyes. Thinking back, a shiver crept through her. There had definitely been more there than met the eye. And it hadn't been good. She wished she had stuck around and paid more attention.

That admission made her thoughts move to the second auction they had attended. Nothing significant had happened that day, but they had met the young mother who *had* stuck around.

In their conversation, Melissa had said she heard the voices of Bob Caldwell and Tanya Williams arguing, something about a fiddler. It didn't make sense, and it probably wasn't important. But Ginger couldn't let it go.

Miles Jarrett said Tanya had operated a booth in the mall flea market. Vendors had been sending buyers to the parking lot to make their buys. Kingpins had been arrested and incarcerated.

As fresh recollections threaded through her mind, a light bulb suddenly flashed.

"She didn't say fiddler," Ginger muttered, facing Jon— as if he were privy to her thoughts.

He glanced over in surprise, and then focused right back at the road. "What are you talking about?"

"Tanya Williams didn't argue with Caldwell about a fiddle or fiddler, as that young woman thought. They were talking about Fielder, the senator."

Jon kept his face aimed forward, but Ginger thought she could hear the mental gears clicking in his head. She filled him in on her thoughts anyhow.

"The senator was running that drug trafficking operation at the mall. Tanya was a vendor there. So, like we suspected, she must have been a seller who didn't get caught. And somehow there's a connection to Caldwell."

Jon nodded. "We have another drug operation, but of a

different nature. Williams worked for Fielder and had a grudge against Caldwell. It could all be coincidence, but I highly doubt it."

"It looks like Caldwell is another kingpin, one who may have been in business with Fielder. If only we could figure out how the diversion operation is being done. It seems so impossible that they can switch out drugs for placebos and leave no trace."

Silent while pulling into the parking lot of the police station, Jon parked and faced her. "Drug counterfeiters often work with package counterfeiters. Some of them are very sophisticated, but no system is completely foolproof. I need to talk to Miles. Do you have any calls you want to make while we're here and you can use an agency phone?"

She welcomed the opportunity. "I'd like to contact Lillian, see how things are going at the office. And I'd like to talk to Erin. Another chat with my parents would also be good."

~

Jon escorted Ginger to an office that wasn't currently being used, borrowed a phone from the captain, and left her to make her contacts with it. He was relieved at knowing she was safe for the moment.

He found Miles in his temporarily assigned office. The face that looked up at Jon's entrance was grim. The agent motioned toward the hallway. "I want to talk to you, but I think you need to bring the chief up to date on your weekend first. Then I want to hear your thoughts before I tell you what I'm getting ready to do."

"Okay, be right back." Jon turned and went down the hall.

"Well, you found trouble, did you?" the chief said when Jon entered his office. He pointed at a chair. "Tell me about it, with details."

Jon outlined the past two days, ending with Ginger's theory about Fielder being involved. "Miles has already talked to the prison warden, and he indicated no knowledge of outside criminal contacts by the senator. Can you check into it any further?"

Ward Billings had been listening intently. Now he leaned forward, arms on his desk. "I'll see if I can push some buttons and dig a little deeper. I understand that our DEA agent has a sting he'd like to put into action. Go let him tell you what he has in mind."

Jon retraced his steps down the hall and faced Miles again.

"Fill me in on your weekend first." Miles nodded at the chair near the desk. "Then I'll tell you what I have in mind."

Jon repeated his tale, feeling a bit like a yoyo, bouncing back and forth between offices and repeating his story. "The chief's going to do some more checking on the senator," he concluded.

Miles frowned. "Do you think Fielder's pulling strings from prison?"

Jon grimaced. "I don't know. He proved he's a clever guy, but I'm not sure how he could be giving orders from behind bars."

"Money," Miles said tersely. "If there's enough money in a guy's stash, he can hire underlings to do about anything he wants done. But we're going to stop this racket." Determination rang in the declaration.

"We know what's being done. Now let's find out how it's done and get the evidence to prove it," Jon challenged.

Over the next half hour, Miles outlined the plan he had already laid out. "The bait is being prepared," he said in conclusion.

Jon stared across the desk. "Ginger wants to go back to work. What do you think?"

Miles shook his head. "She needs to be kept out of sight. Erin would have my hide if anything happened to her. I suspect you would, too."

Jon didn't confirm or deny the gibe. "How long?"

"It depends on the drug manufacturers. They need at least twenty-four hours to produce what we need. You could take Ginger back to Erin's house."

Jon stood. "I'll see if she's agreeable. She doesn't want to put her friend in danger. Whatever we do, I need to pick up some clothes for myself."

"Yeah, you're getting a little rank." Miles smirked as he said it.

Jon ignored him and left to find Ginger pacing the floor in the office where he had left her. She came to meet him, questions in her eyes.

"Let me check my email and phone messages, and then we'll leave," he said quietly. "We'll talk in the car."

Together they walked to his cubicle. He sat behind his desk, and she stood by the door, obviously too restless to use the empty chair by the wall.

He booted his computer and went directly to his email. His eyes rounded when he saw a message from the coroner. He opened it and read.

DNA on the gun and spatula are a match to the sample taken from Dorothy Swanson.

Exultant at finally having proof of something, he forced himself to go through the rest of his messages. It was routine. So while the computer was shutting down, he checked his answering machine. "Call me," Delton Booker's voice ordered.

Jon eased back in the chair and dialed. "You got something?" he asked when Del answered.

"Maybe. I worked last night, and I'm not too wide awake yet."

Jon gave him a moment to collect his thoughts.

"I looked into that case you called me about. Bob Caldwell's ex hasn't been seen or heard from since shortly after their divorce. She was reported missing by her mother, but not until she had been gone for several weeks. Everyone believed she had left town with a man." His tone said the man was a lover.

"I take it you've not learned anymore." Jon inflected it as a question.

"That's all I have for now. I'll let you know if any more information comes to light."

Jon disconnected and spoke to Ginger. "Let's switch your van for my SUV, just in case any bad guys have figured out what we're driving, and then I want to go see Bob Caldwell."

Chapter 15

Ginger waited until they were on the highway before asking, "What can you tell me?"

"More DEA agents are coming, and Miles is setting up a sting operation. On another track, Delton has learned that the mother of Caldwell's first wife reported her missing, but not until she had been gone for several weeks, thinking she had left with a lover. He's still looking into it."

"Back up and tell me more about the sting plan," she said, hungry for details.

He shot a grin over at her. "I think you'll like it. Miles gave me permission to tell you about it. He's having manufacturers of the drugs most sought after by thieves, such as OxyContin and Oxycodone, prepare bait bottles equipped with GPS tracking devices that we can follow to where they're switching the placebos for the real drugs. When the decoys are taken to the courier vehicles, a third-party security firm will notify us."

She was intrigued. "Will these bottles look exactly like the real thing?"

He nodded, keeping his attention focused on the highway. "Each bottle will be weighted and constructed in such a way that, when shaken, they give off a rattling sound, as if pills are inside. When they're removed from a special base, a tracker transmits a signal that can be followed."

"So he's not ready yet," Ginger mused aloud. "He's waiting for the bait to be ready and the extra agents to arrive. It sounds like a good plan, though."

They rode in silence to her apartment, parked in her usual place, and drove away in John's SUV that, thankfully, had not been bothered. Within minutes they were turning onto the narrow street where Caldwell lived. Ginger clutched her purse to her chest as Jon rang the doorbell and waited for a response.

She tensed even more as the door opened and Bob Caldwell himself appeared. This close, she could see the lines in his face. He scowled at sight of them, his lips forming a thin line. "Who are you and what do you want?"

Jon showed his badge. "I have some questions I'd like to ask you. May we come inside?"

The man's mouth moved to speak, but then he hesitated, his gaze raking over them in arrogant assessment. Finally, he backed up and widened the door opening.

They followed him into a living room furnished with dark leather furniture that seemed to reflect the man's cold personality. He settled into a chair and gestured for them to take the sofa. The brief touch of Jon's hand on hers calmed Ginger a tiny bit.

"Well, get your asking done," the man ordered brusquely.

"I'd like you to tell me what you know about Tanya Williams," Jon said, darting a look at Ginger reminding her to not say anything.

"She was a pest," Caldwell snapped, his eyes doing a roll.

A chill raced though Ginger at the iciness of the man.

Jon nodded. "Witnesses have reported seeing her cause disturbances at your places of business. One also heard the two of you arguing."

That seemed to take the man aback, but only for a

moment. "She attended a lot of our auctions. Then she started causing trouble. I guess she was just one of those people who were born to do that."

"You do realize she's dead."

Jon's blunt statement didn't faze the man. "I heard she took a tumble off her balcony. She was probably drunk."

"Was she a heavy drinker?"

He shrugged. "I don't know. I smelled alcohol on her each time she was ranting at the sales, so I assumed she was."

Ginger's heart beat faster, sure the man knew more. But he was an experienced wheeler dealer. They would get no more from him.

Jon changed tactics. "We also understand that your first wife went missing and has never been found."

That did seem to take him off guard. His eyes narrowed. "I guess she did. She found someone else, divorced me, and took off with her new guy. I never asked where they went. I didn't care."

"When did she disappear?"

He made a nonchalant mouth twist. "I never saw her after the divorce papers were signed. She went on with her life, and I went on with mine."

Jon stood, apparently accepting the futility of further questioning and as anxious as she was to get out of there. "We'll see ourselves out," he said, heading to the door.

When they were back in his SUV, he faced Ginger. "It's past noon, but I'd rather not risk taking you into a restaurant. How about picking up a pizza?"

"I'm hungry, but I'm not sure if I can handle food after that." She nodded toward the Caldwell house.

"I'll call in an order. What do you want on your half?"

"Canadian bacon, pepperoni, and mushrooms."

He made the call and then started the engine. By the time they reached the drive-thru window of the pizza place, their order was ready.

When Jon pulled the box inside the window, the aroma

made Ginger's stomach clench. "I don't know how long I can wait," she said, inhaling deeply, her appetite suddenly returned now that they were miles away from Caldwell.

After Jon placed their cold sodas in the drink holders, he swerved into traffic. "If it's not too busy, we could swing around and stop to eat at Sequiota Park."

She nodded.

Five minutes later, Jon pulled into the parking lot of the thirteen-acre paradise just north of Galloway Village. The park that boasted a lagoon where ducks swam, open shelters, picnic tables and grills, restrooms, and playground equipment was one of the few places with public caves. A three-mile walking and fitness trail ran from Galloway to National Court Trail.

As he picked up the pizza box and opened the driver's door, Ginger grabbed the drinks and hopped to the ground on her side of the vehicle. The brisk wind made her glad she had worn a windbreaker with her jeans, tee shirt and sneakers.

They hiked to one of the smaller shelters that had no one near it and placed their containers on the table. Ginger lowered her head while Jon said a brief blessing and asked God to protect them.

They were just finishing the simple meal when Ginger noticed a van pull into the parking lot across the lawn. She thought nothing about it, until another van pulled in and parked beside it. Both vehicles were white—with courier logos on the sides of them.

When the driver of the van nearest them exited and walked around to the other van, she gasped.

"I see him," Jon said, gathering the empty box and cups and tossing them in the trash can at the corner of the shelter. "It's Duke Harrison. I can't tell who it is he's gone to talk to in the other van, but I'm guessing they're both armed. We need to get out of here."

He grabbed Ginger's hand and tugged her toward a tree

to the right of the shelter. Walking briskly, they moved from tree to tree, working their way toward his SUV.

When they reached the side of the vehicle, he eased the passenger door open. "Keep low," he whispered, heading around to the driver's side.

Ginger crawled into the passenger seat, keeping her head down, and shut the door as quietly as she could. As soon as Jon was behind the wheel, he inserted a key in the ignition and started the motor. Then he eased the vehicle backward out of the parking spot. Unfortunately, as he stopped and shifted from reverse to forward, Harrison looked up. His eyes rounded in recognition, and he said something to the other driver. Then he ran to the driver's door of the van he had driven there.

Jon hit the gas pedal, peeled out of the parking lot, and sped toward the highway. As he raced about a mile and whipped right at the intersection where the light was blessedly green, Ginger looked back and saw a white van closing the distance between them.

"I see it," Jon said, steering into the right lane and heading for the interstate. Ginger held her breath as he steered over a lane. The van stayed right behind them, and a sharp intake of breath came from Jon as it whizzed closer.

When it rammed their rear bumper, she was thrown backward against the headrest.

"Hold on," Jon said, laboring to keep the vehicle from skidding off the shoulder of the road.

She clutched the door handle as tightly as she could, her heart thundering.

Once he had the SUV lined out, Jon rammed the gas pedal to the floor.

As the miles passed, she began to breathe easier and loosened her hold on the door handle while he wove through the traffic, doing a basic repeat of their first such escape. When he reached the turnoff to the camp, she eased back in the seat, but still kept her eyes focused on the rearview mirror.

~

After a couple more miles, Jon slowed and rolled into the campground area. As soon as he was parked, he reached for his phone and called his chief.

"Lay low overnight," Billings said when Jon had explained. "I'll have units searching for those drivers, but they're probably gone by now. Let me know if you have more trouble."

"Let's get some rest and go back to town in the morning," Jon said to Ginger after telling her the chief's order. "I'm sorry we don't have food with us this time."

She shrugged. "We just ate. We'll survive."

Jon appreciated her easy acceptance, but wished they had food. At least her bag was still in the back seat. He reached over and grabbed it.

As they walked to the staff cabin, an extra strong gust of wind buffeted their progress. When they reached the building, they found a huge dead limb had blown onto the porch. He set Ginger's bag at the top of the steps and dragged the limb to the side of the building. As he released it, he flinched. A huge splinter had stabbed into his finger and lodged.

"What is it?" Ginger asked, pausing on the bottom step when his breath hissed loudly.

He stepped back close to her and held out his left hand, palm upward, so she could see the splinter. "Can you pull it out?"

"I have tweezers in my purse." She went to get them.

He followed her back up onto the porch and tried to not yelp when she extracted the wooden fragment that felt like a dagger.

"We need to clean it well," she said. "Maybe there's some hydrogen peroxide or rubbing alcohol in the bathroom that we can use to disinfect it."

He watched her tuck the tweezers back into the

manicure kit she had taken from her purse. She started to replace the kit, but paused, staring at the label on it. "What is it?" he asked, studying her troubled expression.

She frowned. "I'm not sure. I bought this at the Morgan Medical Pharmacy. Seeing it made me think of Barry."

Jon wasn't thrilled at the thought of her thinking about that guy, but as he continued to study her expression, he realized that whatever was bothering her was disturbing rather than pleasant. "What's wrong?"

She looked up at him. "I didn't get a good look, but I think the flash I got of that driver in the other van could have been Barry. But why would he have been driving a courier van?"

She didn't say that a van driver job would be beneath Barry, nor did Jon, but he thought it. He pulled out his phone and checked to see if he had internet reception out there. He didn't. So he called Delton. "Can you do some research on a couple of guys and see if you find any connections between them?" he asked when his colleague answered.

"Give them to me."

"Duke Harrison and Barry Morgan."

"I'll get back to you."

"Let's get you inside," Ginger said when he disconnected.

They found some alcohol, and she cleaned his hand with it, using a tissue from her purse. It stung, but he was tough. *Right? Right.*

"Shall we explore the refrigerator at the other building and see if we left anything in it?" he suggested, more for something to do than any expectation of finding food.

They didn't. So they went for a hike. On the way back, Delton called. "Those two guys you asked about attended the same high school. And, get this. The administrator I talked to remembers that they were both very involved in a paintball club."

Jon got the picture. "So the rich snobby kid and the poor

kid from the wrong side of town had a common love for shooting. And now they both have jobs that link to drugs. One dispenses, and the other delivers."

"Right. The rich kid works for his daddy, but the poor kid could have gotten his job with the aid of his old paintball buddy."

"It's only a theory," Jon said, running the scenario through his head. "We need much more."

"We'll get it. Where are you?"

Jon filled him in on their latest incident and their location. "We'll return to town in the morning. Ginger wants to check in on her office and staff, be sure everything is running smoothly, check her email, and be sure that there have been no more incidents with her staff and their clients."

"I'll keep digging," Delton said before ending the call.

Jon met Ginger's questioning look. "Delton found a connection between Duke Harrison and your former boyfriend, Barry Morgan."

"He's not a former boyfriend," she snapped, her eyes shooting sparks. "He was a one date mistake."

He grinned, not happy at being in her bad graces, but pleased at the declaration about Morgan.

"Duly noted," he said, and then continued. "Your mistake and Duke Harrison were high school classmates, and they shared a passion for the sport of paintball."

Her nose and forehead scrunched up in lack of comprehension.

"It's a team shooting sport," he explained. "Players eliminate opponents from the game by hitting them with a dye-filled capsule that breaks on impact. It's called a paintball, and it's shot from a gun powered by compressed air that was originally designed for remotely marking trees and cattle."

"You mean they go out and shoot at one another?" Incredulity laced her tone.

He nodded. "You can't play it on public lands, but it's

commonly played in the woods on the property of team members."

"You mean kind of like army exercises?"

"I suppose you could make such a comparison."

She considered for several moments. "So these guys like guns and shooting at people. Do you think they killed Dottie Swanson?"

"It's possible."

She gave her head several jerky shakes. "I'm having trouble associating Mr. Prim and Proper Barry Morgan with all this. But it sure is looking like he and his old classmate are involved."

Jon nodded. "If they are, I'm guessing that Barry got Duke the courier job for purposes other than just driving a van."

Chapter 16

Early the next morning, a knock on the front door of the building roused Ginger. It was Jon's signal that he was ready to leave.

"Let's grab some breakfast burritos when we hit town," he suggested as he pulled onto the highway minutes later. They did that and had finished eating by the time he pulled in at the strip mall and parked near her office.

Lillian looked up in surprise when they entered. "Well, good morning," she greeted them. "I wasn't expecting you."

"I'm not staying," Ginger said quickly. "I just want you to give me an update on things and tell me how Cheryl, Mrs. Boswell, and Mrs. Haskell are doing."

"They're all doing well. Cheryl told me she had considered quitting, but decided she can't abandon her clients. I know she's especially fond of Mrs. Boswell and feels better now that the woman's bruises are healed. And Katie reports that Mrs. Haskell's condition has improved since getting new prescriptions."

Ginger breathed a sigh of relief. "I want to check my personal email and messages," she explained, heading on into her office.

"I'll wait out here," Jon said, taking a seat.

Ginger hastily opened her email and skimmed through

it, making notes of things to have Lillian check. When finished, she shut down the computer and returned to the reception desk.

"Thanks for everything," she said, handing Lillian the list. "I'll be back as soon as I can."

"I understand," Lillian said, darting a sidelong glance at Jon. She addressed him. "Take care of my girl."

He smiled at Lillian and opened the door for Ginger. When they were outside, Ginger drew to an abrupt halt at recognizing the white haired, suit clad man on the sidewalk. "Why, hello, Pastor Roger," she greeted the minister who had befriended her over a week earlier. "I'm not sure I ever properly thanked you for your help when I was attacked, but please know that I appreciate it very much."

He gave her a quick assessment. "You were very gracious, considering your situation. How badly were you injured?"

"I was more scared than hurt," she said, trying to not let the memory rattle her.

"Glad to hear you're okay. I've wondered about you. Did the police ever catch the person who did it?"

"I'm afraid not," Jon answered for her. "We're still looking for him. Do you mind if I run a couple of names by you and see if you recognize them?"

"Ask away," the minister replied, stepping over against the building as Lillian exited the office and locked the door.

Jon waited until Lillian had left. "Did you know a Mrs. Tanya Williams?"

The pastor frowned in concentration. "I don't recall anyone by that name."

"What about Beverly Caldwell? Does that name ring a bell with you?"

His eyes crinkled as he contemplated for a moment. Then he raised a finger in a give-me-a-moment signal. Moments later, his face brightened.

"I remember now. One evening during prayer requests

at mid-week Bible study, one of our members asked us to pray for a neighbor of hers who had reported her daughter missing. I believe that was the name of the woman who was missing. The neighbor said her daughter was afraid of the husband she had just divorced."

"Do you remember the husband's name?" Ginger asked and waited tensely for a response.

A hand rubbed back and forth over the pastor's mouth and chin, his expression perplexed.

"Could it have been Caldwell?" Jon prodded gently.

The pastor's hand went still. Then he said, "I believe it was. Wait a minute. Are you by chance referring to the city councilman?"

"I'm afraid so," Jon admitted. "His ex-wife has been missing for a long time."

The man's narrowed eyes drilled him. "Do you think you've found her?"

Ginger held her breath, not sure how much Jon would reveal.

"We're following up on the case," he said, being honest, but not providing any details.

The pastor pondered a moment. "Would you like me to talk to that member and see if she can get a picture of the missing woman from that neighbor?"

"I'd appreciate it very much," Jon said, reaching into his pocket and withdrawing a card. "Let me give you this so you can reach me when you've contacted her."

The pastor took the card, glanced at it, and stuck it in his shirt pocket. "You can be sure I will. And I'll continue praying for that family."

~

After they parted company with the minister, Jon escorted Ginger back to his SUV. "I need to go to headquarters and talk to Delton. How about I take you to the church?"

She shook her head. "I don't want to be a bother to the

pastor, or you. Why don't you just take me to my apartment?"

He dipped his chin, giving her a raised brow look. "Are you kidding? There's every chance we're being hunted, and by a smart hunter. You can't stay alone. The church would be occupied, so you wouldn't be alone there."

"The same applies to the police station," she shot back. "I'll stay out of your way while you talk to Delton."

Seeing no point in arguing further, he escorted her back to the SUV and drove to the station. When he pulled into the lot, he spotted a familiar Nissan parked near the entrance.

He sighed inwardly. That pushy reporter, Sadie Miller, was here again, stalking cops with questions that she would then inject with her own slant if they responded.

Pretending ignorance of her presence, he pressed Ginger's right arm for her to move faster, but Sadie had seen them and bolted from her car, waving a hand for attention.

"Hello, Detective Zalinski," she hailed him in her customary manner, hurrying alongside him. "Rumors are flying around town. Is it true that the killer of that pharmacist is after the woman who found her?"

When he realized that Ginger hadn't been recognized by the reporter, he gave her arm a quick squeeze. Understanding, she stayed silent and kept walking.

"No comment," he muttered to the reporter.

"Or is it the killer of that courier driver?" she asked, keeping pace with them. "Can you clear up the story for me?"

Jon slowed his pace just a tad but didn't stop. "As you know, we have someone who handles our media relations. It would be a breach of duties for me to interfere with his job. I'm sure he'll have a press conference scheduled soon. You should attend it to get your information."

The woman scowled. She was the most persistent, and irritating, of those who flocked to the station every time there was word of a major story, or a break in one.

"I'd still rather hear it directly from you, since you're so personally involved," she pressed on—as usual.

"I repeat, it's not my job to provide you with your stories."

Her jaw stiffened.

Moving on, Jon practically dragged Ginger through the doorway and proceeded to the office Delton was currently using.

"I'll sit out here so you can discuss confidential matters privately," Ginger offered, pointing to a chair in the hallway.

He nodded and went on inside the office. Delton sat at a desk, his head bent over a file folder. He looked up, a frown carving lines each side of his mouth. "I was wondering when you'd show up."

"Well, I'm here. What can you tell me that I don't already know?" Jon plopped in the chair.

Delton closed the folder he had been examining. "Not a lot. I was just rereading the files on Caldwell's missing ex-wife. Apparently, their divorce was quite contentious. There were no children, which is probably a blessing if the feeling in my gut proves true."

"You don't think she's alive, do you?"

"I'm afraid not, but I have no proof yet. I've been contacting coroners all over the state and inquiring if they have any unidentified Jane Does."

Jon leaned back and studied him. "You're like a hound after a hare, aren't you? You've gotten a scent of something, and you won't quit until you have answers. That's good."

Delton shrugged. "My mama always said I'm one-track."

"Well, keep tracking."

They chatted for a few more minutes, but nothing put them any closer to knowledge of the woman's whereabouts. They knew a lot about Bob Caldwell now, but nothing that would prove he had anything to do with Beverly's disappearance.

When Delton's phone rang, Jon gave him a good-bye salute and returned to the hallway.

~

Ginger looked up as Jon emerged from the office, and his gaze landed on her. A bit of the tension that had built during her musings over the scary knowledge that someone wanted her dead had dissipated.

"It's nearly lunch time," he said. "How about we pick up some food and eat it at the church? Then you can spend the afternoon there and get some rest."

"You're determined that's where I should stay, aren't you?" she asked, her brow creasing.

"I honestly think it's the best place for right now."

"Okay," she relented, standing. She accompanied him back to his SUV.

"Let's just eat out here," Jon said when he parked at the end of the church parking lot minutes later. Near the entrance were cars that belonged to the pastor and staff members.

She bowed her head while he offered a short blessing before they ate the sandwiches they had picked up on the way. When they were done, Ginger started to open the door, but Jon's hand on her arm brought her to a standstill.

When she turned her head, their gazes locked. "I'm reluctant to leave you," he said, his voice slightly raspy. "But I know it's necessary. I'll come back for you after work, and we'll go to Erin's together. I'll call and tell her I'll bring the meal."

Ginger nodded approval. "She shouldn't have to feed us all the time. You're very thoughtful. And I'll help her with all the work I can."

He placed a finger under her chin and pushed it up to where she couldn't avoid his scrutiny. The next thing she knew, he had drawn her close. Without conscious thought, she clung to him, reveling in the safety and comfort of the embrace and burying her face in the crook of his neck.

His masculine scent cocooned her, teasing her senses as

his hands traced over her back, the caresses sending warmth through her. She lifted her head to meet his gaze.

His eyes darkened with something that made her heart race and her mind reel. She raised a hand and cupped his jaw, letting the bristles of his beard prickle her palm. Not since Aaron's death had she been this close to a man.

Thoughts of Aaron fuzzed her brain, but only for a moment. She drew Jon's head closer until their lips touched and something resembling an electric current jolted through her. Had he felt it?

She started to pull away, but he held her close, his lips suddenly pliant and delicious as they moved over hers. Her head swam, her emotions too scrambled to analyze.

Finally, he broke the kiss and eased back to stare at her, his handsome face filled with an expression of perplexity to match her own.

She blinked. How could that have felt so right?

He cupped her cheek, smiling. "I think it's time I take you inside."

When she was upstairs in the safe room, Ginger landed in a heap on the bed, too addled to think clearly. Her feelings for Jon had escalated beyond reason or understanding. Had she betrayed Aaron?

Lord, please help me, she prayed under her breath. *I know I've ignored You and blamed You, and here I am asking You for help. Please forgive me.*

As she went quiet and limp, a memory from the Bible came to mind.

For if you forgive men their trespasses, your heavenly Father will also forgive you.

She moaned. Yes, she had made mistakes. And now that she reflected, she realized that God had forgiven her.

But she had not forgiven the man whose drunk driving had caused Aaron's death.

Tears tracking down her cheeks, she laid there staring up at the ceiling and accepted what she had to do.

"I forgive you, Mr. Hawkins," she mouthed in a whisper. The man was no longer under her judgment. The matter was between the man and God.

As the weight of bitterness lifted from her, Ginger swiped at her cheeks and gulped at the clog in her throat. She felt lighter, clearer, more ready to face life.

As she continued to lie there, drifting, Jon's face returned to mind. Although Aaron was gone, Jon was here. And he had become the center of her world, all she wanted.

A bigger picture began to form.

She had existed in her bitter state for years. And then, with finding Martha's body, everything had seemed to go completely berserk. Now she began to see the entire sequence of events with fresh vision.

Through it all, Jon had been brought into her life. Good had come from bad.

Had there been a master plan, one designed by God?

She didn't know all the answers, and her common sense warned her to be careful. But her heart wanted it to be so.

She closed her eyes.

Chapter 17

That afternoon, feeling less than energetic after the tiring day, Jon entered the conference room at police headquarters for the briefing Miles had scheduled, Ginger at his side. Her presence had only been allowed at Jon's request because of her deep involvement in the case and his reluctance to leave her alone anywhere. Half a dozen newly arrived DEA agents, plus several of their own deputies, occupied folding chairs that had been brought in for extra seating. The mood was all business as Miles called the meeting to order and went right to the main topic.

"The bait bottles are ready and are being transported to the warehouse for pickup by the couriers. We have maps of all their routes, and you guys will be stationed at various points throughout the city. The plan is for the bottles to start moving tomorrow morning. As they're picked up by the couriers they'll be tracked. If any courier deviates from his or her route, whoever is nearest that location will tail the rogue."

Jon caught Ginger's nod. She had been listening intently and apparently liked the plan.

"Pharmacists have been notified about the bait battles," Miles continued.

Ginger gasped, and her head whipped around to face

Jon.

"What's wrong?" Miles asked from the front of the room.

Ginger hesitated, her eyes asking Jon if she should answer. He nodded.

"I don't have any proof, but I think the pharmacist at Morgan Pharmacy may be involved in the operation," she said. "That means he'll know what you're doing."

"What's his name?"

When she named Barry, Miles promptly grabbed his phone and dialed his agency contact, motioning with a hand for everyone to sit tight. "Can you put a stop on one of those pharmacy notifications?" he asked moments later.

When Miles winced, Jon's heart sank. Were they blown out of the saddle before getting hold of the reins? He watched as Miles waited. When he nodded at whatever he was hearing, the expression on his face made the tension ease a bit in Jon's neck. The room echoed with silent anticipation.

"Okay, thanks," Miles said, disconnecting and focusing on the group. "The Morgan Medical Pharmacy has been deleted from the list of notifications. Mike also deleted the pharmacists on the route formerly driven by Dottie Swanson—as a precaution in case one of them is involved."

"So now we wait," Jon said quietly to Ginger as the meeting was dismissed. "And pray all goes according to plan."

With a hand behind her waist, he steered them toward Miles. "Do you have a particular assignment for me?" he asked the agent.

Miles nodded. "I'm going to put an agent on stakeout to watch that Morgan Pharmacy tomorrow and be ready to tail him the minute he's loaded, but my gut says that place needs to be watched starting now. If I have someone there throughout the night, can you be there before dawn in the morning? We don't want anyone slipping in early and alerting the guy that we're onto him."

"I think he already knows that, but I doubt the person he's working for does. So he'll probably stick to his schedule."

"May I sit with Jon on stakeout?"

Ginger's question claimed their attention.

"It's not a good idea," Miles said without hesitation. "But I'll leave it to Jon and his boss."

Jon read the look of determination on her face. He could leave her with Erin, but would she stay there and not slip out to spy on them? Knowing Erin's history, he was afraid to leave the two of them alone. "If I talk to the chief and tell him you'll stay in the car, will you promise to do that?" he asked her.

Her eyes said she didn't like it, but she nodded. "I'll stay."

"I'll make the call, and then go check out an unmarked vehicle."

"When that's done, meet me at Erin's for supper," Miles instructed.

~

"What time do you plan to relieve whoever's on stakeout?" Ginger asked Jon as they sat at the table with Erin and Miles, enjoying dishes of banana pudding after polishing off a pot roast, potatoes and carrots Erin had cooked in her new instant pot.

He glanced briefly at Miles. "I told the officer who's on duty tonight that I'll relieve him at four in the morning."

"I have some bakery cinnamon rolls you can take with you," Erin offered. "And I'll dig out the thermoses so Ginger can fill them with coffee."

"You're too good to us," Ginger scolded, a smile on her face. She reached for her tea glass, but paused when Jon's phone rang.

He stood and left the table, answering as he went. "Zalinski."

His voice carried from the living room, but not clearly.

Five minutes later, he returned to the kitchen. He was smiling. "That was Pastor Roger. He said he has the picture of Caldwell's missing ex-wife that he promised to try to get for us. I told him we'll come get it. Then I called Delton. He says his contacts with coroners from all over the state have resulted in three of them saying they have Jane Doe cases. All three sent him copies of photos from their files, and the pictures are in his desk drawer at work if we want to see them."

"You bet we do." Ginger downed the last bite of her pudding and washed it down with tea.

"I'm finishing mine, too," Jon declared as he took her dish to the sink with his.

"Don't worry about the dishes," Miles said. "I'll help Erin load the dishwasher and clean up the kitchen."

They thanked him and hurried to the living room. Ginger grabbed her purse from the coffee table as they passed it, practically running outside to Jon's SUV.

Minutes later, Jon drove up to the parsonage next to the church that Roger Hampton pastored. The man met them at the door, an envelope in his hand. He handed it to Jon. "I hope this helps."

"We do, too." Ginger suddenly felt foolish for having followed Jon to this house. He was on police business. She was just a tagalong. But she had acted on impulse, anxious to find answers. And she liked the pastor. "Thanks for being so willing to help," she said, happy to see him again.

They returned to the SUV, and Jon drove to the police station. He greeted the officer on night desk duty as he escorted Ginger to Delton's cubicle and opened the desk drawer. He extracted three photos and placed them in a row on the desk. Then he opened the envelope from Pastor Roger and placed it near them.

The morgue photos were hard to look at. The faces of those unclaimed women bore signs of violence and deterioration. But there was no doubt as to which one matched the photo Pastor Roger had supplied.

"I'll text Delton and tell him we're leaving these two together for him to follow up on when he can," Jon said, sliding the matching ones into an envelope and marking an X on it.

They returned to Erin's house and utilized her guest bed and sofa to get some rest. Ginger rested, but was unable to sleep much.

~

Jon wasn't surprised to find Ginger already up when he left the sofa well before dawn the next morning. Erin had left their promised rolls on the cabinet.

"I have the coffee made." Ginger indicated the thermoses beside the rolls.

Minutes later, they were in the unmarked car Jon had checked out the day before, driving in silence to the clinic where Barry's pharmacy was located.

Jon drove up behind the officer on duty and signaled that he could leave. They were at the far side of the parking lot, shielded by the trees lining it, and Jon kept the tinted car windows closed. The coffee and rolls served not only as nourishment, but as a diversion from the awareness of being alone in the vehicle with Ginger beside him.

Eating occupied them as they watched the sun rise. The second day of April had arrived cool and damp, with the wind still blowing slightly.

Suddenly Jon put his thermos down and reached for the binoculars he had placed in the glove compartment. Beside him, Ginger leaned forward in the seat, also staring at the van that had just pulled in at the clinic.

"I think I saw a car pull into the back lot where employees park," she breathed tensely. "It's too early for the clinic to open, unless someone has a special appointment— or something," she added vaguely.

Jon positioned the binoculars over his eyes and watched the driver of the van emerge and walk to the entrance, his back to them. Moments later the door opened, and the driver entered the building.

"What now?" Ginger asked.

"Our job is only to observe, and report anything unusual." He called Miles. "I think that driver is Duke Harrison," he reported after explaining about the early arriving van and someone entering the clinic from the rear to admit him.

"I'm headed that way. Sit tight."

As Jon disconnected, Ginger gasped. "He's leaving. That notification to delete Barry from the pharmacists to be notified of the plan must not have been sent in time to stop him. He must have gotten it, and they know what's up and are making some kind of move. Duke's leaving."

As a GPS signal sounded, Jon started the motor. He couldn't just sit here and let Duke be without a tail. "Call Miles. Tell him Duke's on the move, and we're following."

As she grabbed her phone, he pulled into the road at a distance behind the van. When she had made the call, he said, "Check that map of Duke's route. It's the top one of those printouts." He indicated the papers on the dashboard.

He had followed the van for a little over a mile when it made an unexpected right turn into a business district.

"He may be headed for their diversion site," Ginger said, straining forward against the seat belt while peering at the map in her hand. "He just left his route."

Not sure what he was expecting, Jon was still surprised when the van pulled in at a garage. The driver got out and entered the place. "Maybe he has vehicle trouble," he speculated, pulling next to the curb half a block away.

He dialed Miles again, his nerves stretching paper thin. As Miles responded, he had opened his mouth to speak when a blast sounded, and a bullet shattered the driver's window and hit the steering wheel gripped in his left hand.

Chapter 18

As Ginger's breath wheezed in and out of her lungs in nearly airless gasps, she looked over and saw Jon slumped back against the seat. Blood colored the steering wheel and the front of his jacket.

A car came roaring up beside them and screeched to a halt. Miles leaped from it and ran to their vehicle. "Are you okay?" he yelled, yanking the door open.

"I'm okay," Jon said from between clenched teeth, pulling upright and gripping one hand in the other. "The bullet only hit my hand."

"It was a trap," Ginger said as bits of the picture floated into focus. "Barry must be at the head of this mess."

The idea bewildered her. He had everything money could buy. So why did he want more—so badly that he would steal, and even kill, for it?

She tugged Jon's hand toward her for examination. There was a hole in the flesh between his thumb and index finger. She grabbed her purse and pulled out the small packet of tissues she carried. Seeing all that blood made her realize just how much Jon meant to her. She loved him.

"I'll call an ambulance." Miles already had his phone in his hand.

"No," Jon protest loudly. "It's only a flesh wound.

There's no time. Duke must have gone out the back of that garage and circled around to a vantage point somewhere over there." He pointed across the street.

"Do you think the operation is blown?" Miles asked, watching as Ginger pressed the tissues against the blood flow.

"I'm not sure," Jon said, gritting his teeth as she pressed on the wound. "Duke and Barry clearly are working together, but the timing of all this is wrong. There's no question they were up to something, but Duke may have spotted us as he arrived and put off whatever it was to follow up on his last attempt to shoot us. He has to know we're onto him."

Before Miles could concur or disagree, his phone rang. He answered, made short acknowledgments of whatever he was hearing, and then disconnected.

"One of our agents said he's following the signal of a van that just deviated from its route. And another agent has the same thing happening. I need to catch up to those guys."

"I'll take one of them while you get the other," Jon said. "Tell me how to find it. This car may be damaged, but it's still drivable."

Miles gave him the information and raced back to his own car.

Ginger carefully brushed glass fragments from the seat as Jon started the engine.

He glanced over at her. "I have to leave you here."

"No way. Drive." She pointed at the road.

Rather than waste time arguing, he gunned the vehicle forward, steering mostly with his right hand and resting the injured one on the wheel. "I need you to enter the GPS location Miles just gave me."

As the car shot onto the highway, she punched in the coordinates. The early morning traffic was starting to pick up as people headed to their jobs. And the wind blew small fragments of glass through the shattered holes in the windshield and side window. Ginger reached up and wiped at the windshield with a tissue.

"I think that's our agent," she said a minute later, pointing up ahead at a sedan being driven by a man she thought she recognized as the blond agent who had sat near them at the briefing.

Jon steered into the center lane and edged up closer to the vehicle. When the driver glanced over, he raised his bloody hand and mouthed, "I'm a cop." The plain-clothes agent nodded understanding, his gaze taking in the shattered window and hole in the windshield. He beckoned for them to follow him.

When the lead car gave a right signal, Ginger held her breath as Jon followed the agent off the interstate. After a couple of turns, the agent stopped at the edge of a city block of storage units. A courier van was parked down at the end of the row, in front of a huge unit.

Jon parked at a distance, behind a row of parked cars, and pulled out his binoculars. Ginger reached over with the last of her tissues and wiped at the blood on his hand. "You have to get that properly treated."

"I will, when we're done here." He raised the field glasses to his eyes and peered across the lot. "That van is being loaded, or I assume reloaded," he muttered. "They've made the switch."

He put the glasses down and grabbed his phone. "I'm calling Miles," he said while dialing. "That van is about ready to leave."

Miles answered, his voice carrying to her. "My agent just called. We'll intercept."

"Okay, just wanted to be sure you're aware. The problem is we don't know who's in that storage building. Do you want to raid it now?"

Ginger strained to follow both sides of the conversation. "I'm at the edge of the lot," Miles replied, his voice coming through fairly clear. "We need to know more, make sure we nail whoever is behind this operation. So for right now I want you to just sit tight and observe. My agent will tail this driver when he leaves and arrest him with his load of goods."

"Which is happening right now," Jon said.

"Another van has just entered the lot," Ginger whispered.

"You second van is arriving," Jon relayed to Miles.

"An agent is behind it," Miles responded. "Gotta go."

Ginger thought her muscles would snap from the tension running through her as they sat and watched the second driver being met by two men who emerged from the storage unit and immediately began to unload the van. Minutes after carrying the packages inside, they reemerged with identical looking ones and proceeded to load them.

"I've spotted the agent," Jon said, aiming his binoculars at the perimeter of the huge lot. "What we're seeing tells me the placebo packages were ready, and they're just making the switches. As soon as they're done, the driver will return to his route. That means they have someone supplying order information. I wonder how those drivers will feel when the DEA agents intercept and arrest them with the goods in their possession."

The wry comment eased Ginger's tension just a tad. "As scary as the thought is, I'd kind of like to see their faces when it happens."

Jon darted a grin over at her. "Me, too."

They sat there and watched the van roll away, the agent following at a distance. Minutes later, Jon's phone rang. He answered, grunted short responses, and disconnected. "Miles says they have those two drivers in custody, but they're keeping everything as quiet as possible. He wants to stake out this place overnight, put pole cameras on utility poles, and watch for any action. I sure wish I could see what's inside that building."

"Maybe they'll get pictures of tomorrow morning's exchange." Excitement pulsed in Ginger at the idea. "The head honchos have to be caught. If they're not, they'll just move their operation and hire new minions."

~

Jon nodded, his mind racing. He called Miles back. "I'm going to stick around here. If you're okay with it, I'd like to enter that building and have a look around once it empties and it gets dark. I'll ask the chief to get us a search warrant and have it delivered to me."

"I'd like a look, too," Miles responded. "Now that we've arrested those drivers, we have to move faster. We'll have those cameras in place within the next hour. Then, when the building is empty, you and I will go in together."

"What about Ginger? I don't want to leave her alone out here."

There was a pause. "I know she's too much like Erin to send her home and expect her to stay there. Can you get one of your officers to stay with her?"

"I'll call Delton."

"See you in a few."

Jon put the phone down and faced Ginger. "We're going to stay and keep watch while Miles has surveillance cameras put in place. Now that we've seen evidence of criminal activity, he and I are going to see if we can enter that building and look around. You will stay out here with another officer."

He raised a hand when she started to protest. "It's not negotiable. This is a dangerous police matter, and you're a civilian. I'll have Delton come and let you sit in his car with him—out of range—or you can be taken to Erin's."

She nodded. "Thanks for that much."

He called the chief and arranged for a warrant. Then he called Delton, and they agreed that Delton would pick up the warrant, bring it to him later that afternoon, and then stick around to guard the building while he and Miles were inside.

Minutes later, he and Ginger watched a utility truck pull to the curb across the street and a man go up an electric pole.

Within minutes, cameras were in place on each side of the building.

By the time Delton arrived, Jon was antsy. They were watching the parking lot empty and the sun sink beyond the horizon when he saw Miles pull into the lot. He found himself reluctant to have Ginger leave when Delton took her to his car. Being with her had become way too important to him.

He grabbed the high beam flashlight Delton had brought him and slid out of the unmarked police car. He hiked around the perimeter of the lot to the rear of the unit of interest, where Miles met him from the other direction, also carrying a large flashlight.

"I have the warrant," Jon said as Miles made quick work of the lock. He raised the door just enough for them to duck under it, and then lowered it behind them. Once inside, they switched on their bright lights and began a slow walk around the large room that proved to be a well-equipped drug manufacturing lab.

"This confirms most of our suspicions," Miles commented. "And all those tables of containers and labels say it's big. Someone knowledgeable is running this."

Jon beamed his light toward the far wall. "There's a door between this and the next unit."

"As soon as we get pictures of this, we'll check it out. Shine your light on a section at a time and let me take shots of it with my phone."

As soon as he had enough pictures to satisfy him, Miles headed for the connecting door. "Guess what," he said, looking back at Jon and grinning. "It's open."

Jon followed him inside. "It's a packaging setup," he said, holding his light aloft and sweeping the beam over the room. More pictures?"

"You bet. Then let's get out of here."

As soon as they were done, they hurried outside, closed and locked the door, and beat it to their vehicles.

Chapter 19

Jon flexed the tender muscles in his hand. They had stopped by the emergency room last night and had it treated and bandaged. Even though Ginger was a former EMT, the fact that it was a gunshot wound meant it had to be properly documented and reported.

Although sore, his hand was the least of his worries right now. His concern was Ginger's presence in another unmarked car with Delton, parked at the far edge of the huge parking lot. She had hinted at watching this morning's raid from her own car. Rather than risk her not being able to resist the temptation to do that, he had again asked Delton to serve as her bodyguard.

Jon settled back in the seat of a different car, one without gunshot damage, to watch as cars began to trickle into the lot and park. Some of the people who emerged went to units where vendors had their goods on display. Others drove around to the back of the units, presumably employees or owners getting ready to conduct sales, put things in storage, or haul them away.

Blended in with the traffic were vehicles driven by DEA agents and officers sent by the police chief, rolling across the lot and going different directions. Jon knew that each of them had been provided with photos of Duke Harrison,

Barry Morgan, and Bob Caldwell.

Everyone waited, hoping to catch the thieves in action.

Less than an hour later, a courier van pulled into the lot and drove to that last double size unit. As soon as the driver emerged, two guys came to meet him and help unload the van. Minutes later, they returned and reloaded it.

As they did, the radio crackled. "Move in now," Miles said loudly.

In rapid coordination officers approached the building at a run from different parts of the lot. Some surrounded the van, while others entered the building. Jon veered to join the ones breaching the drug lab.

Weapons drawn, Miles shouted as they entered, "Don't move. DEA."

Jon scanned the room quickly—and spotted Bob Caldwell circling it at a run toward the rear exit. He took off after the man, weaving around the tables piled with containers and lab paraphernalia, gaining ground on the fleeing criminal.

In a burst of speed, Jon lunged toward the door Caldwell jerked open and slammed a palm against it. As it slammed shut, Caldwell whirled, a gun raised in his hand.

In a flash, Jon swung his own gun and caught Caldwell in the jaw. The man yelped and fell backward, grabbing for a handhold and finding none. His gun fired wildly, and an overhead light fixture shattered.

Jon landed across the man, pinning him to the floor, and then cuffing his hands behind his back before snatching up his dropped weapon. As he stood and yanked Caldwell to his feet, another officer approached and grabbed him by a forearm.

At that moment the voice of an officer who was watching the cameras came over Jon's shoulder radio. "I just spotted Morgan on camera. His features are mostly hidden by a cap, but I'm sure it's him. He's escaping around the end of the building."

"I'll take care of this one," the officer gripping Caldwell's arm said.

Jon nodded and headed out the exit Caldwell had attempted to escape through. "Give me directions," he said into his radio as he ran alongside the back of the building.

"He's running around the end of the lot, heading south."

Jon's heart leaped into his throat. Delton and Ginger were parked over that way. He ran faster, and spotted Morgan running along the edge of the lot. Suddenly the guy slowed a bit, staring at something. Then he resumed his speed—veering toward Delton's vehicle.

~

Ginger sat rigid in the car seat, staring across the expanse of paved surface inhabited by a smattering of parked vehicles. Suddenly she spotted a lone figure running toward them. She squinted, trying to make out his features. The long brimmed baseball cap he wore obscured his face, but she could see that he carried a gun.

When he paused, and then headed around behind them, her breath hitched.

"Stay here," Delton ordered, opening the driver's door.

As he stepped out of the car, the gunman made a burst of speed and rounded to the passenger side where Ginger sat. When he yanked the door open, her breath caught at the sight of Barry Morgan.

In her peripheral vision, she saw Delton moving toward the front of the car just as Barry grabbed her arm and yanked her out of the seat. He pressed a gun against her neck.

"You should have stayed out of things," he hissed, hooking an arm around her shoulders and dragging her backward.

In shock, Ginger stared at Delton, who had halted at the front bumper, as yet unnoticed by Barry. "All I did was find Martha after Dottie killed her," she said, making conversation in a desperate attempt to distract Barry. Across the lot, she spotted Jon, bent low and weaving around behind the parked cars.

"Now you're going to find us a way out of here." Barry pulled her another step backward. "If you want to stay alive, you'll do it."

"Did you kill Dottie?" she asked, realizing he couldn't escape, and she would end up dead when he comprehended that.

"No," he screamed in her ear. "Duke did that. She was a screw-up and had to be taken out."

"But you were there," she yelled, stumbling as he prodded her to move faster.

"So what," he raged, jerking her so hard her shoulder wrenched. She gritted her teeth against the pain. "You're so high and mighty. How does it feel to know you're about to die?"

"You said or did something to get your pals to keep attacking me, didn't you?" she accused in a guttural breath as the idea flashed in her brain.

He uttered an evil sound and gave her another shove, dragging her with him toward a white van. "I might have told them you knew enough to blow everything wide open," he grunted.

Suddenly he whirled, raised his gun, and fired behind them. She twisted her head enough to see Delton, who had been following them, fall back. At the same time, she spotted movement through the windows of a parked vehicle that told her cops were closing in on them.

Barry also saw something and glanced back at Delton, momentarily distracted. Seizing the moment, Ginger reached up and grabbed the arm that encircled her neck. Then she clamped her mouth down on it and bit—hard. Barry screamed and swung a fist at her, striking her head and knocking her down.

From behind them, Jon raced forward and grabbed Barry's gun hand, spun him around, and then yanked his arms behind him.

Ginger fell to her knees, the wrenched shoulder failing to support her, and toppled over onto it. The pain of that, plus the blow to her head, scattered her senses.

Then gentle hands were cupping her face, and Jon's eyes, full of fear and concern, stared down at her. He brushed a hand over her face and pushed hair from her forehead.

"I'm okay," she said breathlessly, anxious to reassure him.

"Thank you, Lord," he breathed against her cheek. Then he helped her to her feet and escorted her away from where Delton was cuffing Barry.

"Are you hurt?"

"My shoulder was wrenched when he jerked me out of the car." She rested that arm across her abdomen and didn't mention the blow to her head.

"Should I call an ambulance?"

"No."

"As soon as we have this mess cleared away, I'll take you to the ER and have it x-rayed." His phrasing made it another non-negotiable.

Chapter 20

Jon's gut clenched as he left the interrogation room and headed for the conference room. That experience when it looked like Barry would kill Ginger kept replaying in his mind. During that moment, his blood had run cold, and he recognized the truth he had been denying to himself. He loved Ginger and would have given anything to save her, including his own life.

The knowledge had given him the strength to act, but now he had cold feet. He didn't dare think she could return his feelings. Or have any idea what he would do about it if she did. Some brave detective he was.

He needed to stay focused on his job. With that in mind, he entered the room where the chief, Miles, and Delton waited for him.

"Any luck?" the chief asked from the head of the conference table.

Jon nodded and took a seat next to Delton. "Getting shot and nearly dying scared Duke. Add to that the fact that he doesn't want to take all the blame, and he's talking."

"So who did what?" came from Miles.

"According to Duke, Barry is the pharmacist for the drug ring. He coordinates the manufacturing of the placebos, oversees the packaging, and provides inside information on what drug orders to divert. Duke is a driver who doubles as a hit man when needed."

"Duke admits he killed Dottie?"

Jon nodded. "It's beyond my understanding what some people will do for money."

Delton raised a finger for attention. "I've been researching all I can find about the people involved in this case. Barry has a wife with tastes and spending habits as lavish as his. And I just learned that he has a gambling habit."

"What else have you found out about Bob Caldwell, the city councilman?" Miles asked.

Delton grimaced. "He killed his first wife. After that Jane Doe was identified as her, I read the coroner's report from the morgue that had her body. She was found by a crew of utility workers behind some bushes off the highway where they were working. I went there and searched the area. Eventually I found her car in a gully about a half mile south of the dump site."

Jon frowned. "Do you think he abducted her in her own car?"

"That's my theory," Delton said, tapping a finger on the conference table. "There's evidence that at some point she was in the trunk."

"What kind of evidence?" Jon and Miles asked simultaneously. They exchanged grins.

Delton produced one as well. "I found her cell phone."

Jon noted the lines of fatigue in the officer's face. "Were you up all night working on this?"

Delton's response was a shrug. "More like the last couple of nights."

"Did you get anything off the phone?"

"It took some doing, and the help of some good technicians who finally revived it and accessed her voice mail. Her last message was to her mother, who never got it because her phone had died while she was in the hospital having surgery, and she didn't replace the phone until weeks later and never checked her voice mail. Anyhow, the message from Beverly said Bob was going to kill her because she had told him she would tell the police about his drug business if he didn't stop harassing her. Then she screamed, and the phone went dead. The mother says Bob was enraged over their divorce settlement."

The chief's head bobbed. "That sounds like evidence that will make the prosecutor very happy. Did you find anything else useful in the phone?"

"Not the phone, but in the phone records," Delton qualified. "I didn't get access to those until late yesterday. After tracking numbers most of the night, I found two calls to the prison."

"Caldwell talked to the senator with her phone?" Jon asked, hope boosting his excitement level.

Delton nodded. "I called the prison warden. He called back just a while ago and said he checked their records closer and talked with some guards. He confirmed that the two did communicate."

"So Caldwell and Fielder are connected," Jon muttered in satisfaction. Then he noticed the gleam in Delton's eyes. "There's more, isn't there?"

His grin widened. "After I chatted with Megan Lathrop, the former employee who had an affair with Caldwell—and you talked to earlier—saying she overheard mention of an overseas account in a phone conversation, I started digging into his financial records."

"You found a foreign account," Jon breathed, hardly able to believe what he was hearing.

"I did. And the senator's name is also on it."

"So the senator has been a silent partner all along."

"Tanya Williams worked for him at the mall and should have been satisfied that she wasn't caught," Delton continued. "But as time passed, she resented Caldwell because his drug business flourished while the one at the mall was shut down. I'm guessing she wanted to work for Caldwell, and he wouldn't use her. I think he grew tired of her harassment and got rid of her. That's the confession I'm hoping to get after we leave here."

The chief leaned forward, his gaze locked on Delton. "Officer Booker, you've just earned yourself a steady position working cold cases—if you're interested," he added in a hopeful tone.

Delton considered for a moment. Then he grinned. "I think I am."

The meeting ended, and they left the room. To Jon's surprise, he found Ginger sitting out front when he entered the lobby. He wasn't ready to face her.

He loved her. But he wasn't husband material. Look what had happened to his parents.

He and Ginger had separate lives and would return to them.

Never kiss again.

And she might not feel the way he did.

"Are you waiting for someone?" he asked inanely. Awkwardly.

"Yes." She rose from her chair and came to his side. "I want the update you promised."

He glanced around the busy room. "Let's go outside."

She walked out the door with him. No one else was near the building, so he moved over to a spot near the wall and gave her a quick summary of what progress had been made.

"So the case is settled. What will you do now?" she asked when he finished.

"My job is dangerous," he began, hoping she understood that their time together was over. "There are other cases begging for my attention. Now you can return to your duties."

He started to say more, but was at a loss for words. Then, in the most insane and lacking of forethought moment of his life, he lowered his head and kissed her with an intensity that shook his world.

Then he pulled back and walked away.

~

When Ginger returned to work, she found everything in good order. Lillian had done well in her absence, but seemed thrilled to have Ginger back in charge.

As the days passed, she stored the memory of Jon's kiss deep inside her and poured her energy into work. But, even in the midst of a mountain of duties, clients, and workers to see to, she experienced loneliness unlike anything she would have thought possible.

Then one day she looked up from her computer screen, and her heart flew into overdrive.

"Wha …what are you doing here?" she stammered, staring at the sight of Jon standing in her doorway. She swallowed, afraid she was dreaming.

He gave her a somewhat sheepish grin. "I lost something. Do you have time to go to the campground and help me look for it?"

"When?" She didn't even consider refusing.

"As soon as you can leave here."

She didn't have to look at the clock. It was ten minutes until quitting time. "I can go now," she said, shoving papers into her desk, shutting down her computer, and taking her purse from a storage cabinet. The April weather was warm enough that she hadn't worn a jacket with her light blue pant suit.

"I'm leaving now," she informed Lillian as they headed across the reception area.

Lillian grinned, her brows lifting. "Have fun."

Jon's quietness as he drove made Ginger uneasy. She could tell he had something heavy on his mind. The hope that had risen when he appeared was fading. He seemed all business, intent on finding whatever he had lost.

When he pulled in at the camp and parked, he exited the SUV and rounded it to meet her at the passenger door. "I'd like to take a walk—if you don't mind." He seemed tense. Jumpy.

Ginger placed her hand in his outstretched one, taking a quick breath and inhaling the heady scent of his aftershave. "I thought you said you were coming to look for something you lost."

He faced her more directly. "I lost something, but not at this camp."

She frowned, confused. "Oh? What do you mean?"

He took a deep breath, as if steeling himself. "I lost my heart soon after we met. To you. And I'm hoping to …well, talk about it."

Ginger inhaled deeply and released the breath slowly, but it didn't calm her or slow the racing pace of her heart. Tears of joy stung the back of her eyes.

"My job can be too dangerous, the hours are unpredictable, and I'll never be rich," he enumerated slowly, and then rushed on. "I know you deserve better than me, and you're grieving your lost fiancé. But I'll wait if you'll spend time with me and see if you can learn to love me."

"Jon," she said quickly, placing a finger over his mouth. "Listen to me."

He paused, as if afraid to hear what she had to say.

"You're patient and hardworking, the kind of man any woman would be honored to have. If you're worried that you could end up like your parents, don't. There's no way. You're dedicated to helping people, you love your job and the Lord—and I don't have to learn to love you."

His eyes rounded, a twitch tugging at the corners of his mouth. "You don't?"

"I loved Aaron, but I love you just as much." She went up on her tiptoes and touched her lips to his, leaning into his chest.

He pulled back and peered down at her. "Enough to marry me?"

She nodded. "Yes. I know there are some risks in what

you do, but you don't have to choose between me and your job. If we face problems, and I'm sure we will, we'll work through them together. I want to share life with you."

The threatening smile broke free, wide and joyous. Then he bent his head and pressed a tender kiss to her lips.

She returned it wholeheartedly, her heart overflowing with pure joy.

They never did get around to taking that walk.

The End

Can detective Delton Booker
solve the cold case of Quincy
Clark's missing parents before whoever
is trying to kill her is successful?
Find out in Cold Case Complicity.
Coming soon.

BOOKS by Helen Gray

ROMANCES

Ozark Sweetheart
Ozark Reunion
Ozark Wedding

Bandit Bride
Prairie Bride

Bootheel Bride
Bootheel Bachelor
Bootheel Betrothal

Show Me Love
Heartland Illusions
Mozark Vision
Missouri Catch

Schoolhouse Justice
Small Town Injustice
Workplace Danger

Paige's Proposal
Brooke's Bargain
Haley's Hero
Kelsey's Keeper

NOVELLAS

River Town Romance
(2 in 1, Hawthorn Hope & Tree of Hope)

Love Blooms
(2 in 1, Pasque Plight & Black-Eyed Susan's Secret)

Mother Road Matches
(2 in 1, Shamrock Ruby & Dream Team)

Secrets in the Park

Gift Bride (Sequel to Dodge City Duos)

A Time to Love

MYSTERIES

Educated in Murder
Preyed in Murder
Coached in Murder
Rivaled in Murder
Keyed in Murder
Tutored in Murder